Praise for

Maybe He Just Likes You

"Mila is a finely drawn, sympathetic character dealing with a problem all too common in middle school. Readers will be cheering when she takes control! An important topic addressed in an age-appropriate way."

—Kimberly Brubaker Bradley, author of
Newbery Honor Book *THE WAR THAT SAVED MY LIFE*

"In *Maybe He Just Likes You*, Barbara Dee sensitively breaks down the nuances of a situation all too common in our culture—a girl not only being harassed, but not being listened to as she tries to ask for help. This well-crafted story validates Mila's anger, confusion, and fear, but also illuminates a pathway towards speaking up and speaking out.
A vital read for both girls and boys."

—Veera Hiranandani, author of
Newbery Honor Book *THE NIGHT DIARY*

"Mila's journey will resonate with many readers, exploring a formative and common experience of early adolescence that has too often been ignored. Important and empowering."

—Ashley Herring Blake, author of
Stonewall Children's & Young Adult Honor Book
IVY ABERDEEN'S LETTER TO THE WORLD

"*Maybe He Just Likes You* is an important, timeless story with funny, believable characters. Mila's situation is one that many readers will connect with. This book is sure to spark many productive conversations."
—**Dusti Bowling,** author of
INSIGNIFICANT EVENTS IN THE LIFE OF A CACTUS

"In this masterful, relatable, and wholly unique story, Dee shows how one girl named Mila finds empowerment, strength, and courage within. I loved this book."
—**Elly Swartz,** author of
SMART COOKIE and ***GIVE AND TAKE***

"*Maybe He Just Likes You* is the perfect way to jump-start dialogue between boy and girl readers about respect and boundaries. This book is so good. So needed! I loved it!"
—**Paula Chase,** author of
SO DONE and ***DOUGH BOYS***

Praise for

Everything I Know About You

"[Tally's] passionate impulse to protect her friends is immediately sympathetic, as is her growing understanding of both herself and her classmates. . . . A poignant and often hilarious slice of middle-grade life."
—*Kirkus Reviews*

"Dee (*Star-Crossed*) sensitively portrays Tally's fears about being left behind as friends change, as well as the signs and impact of the anorexia Ava is hiding. Readers will root for big-hearted Tally, whose willingness to speak her truth makes for honest and engaging narration."
—*Publishers Weekly*

"Ava's struggle with anorexia is portrayed with care and makes an important subject accessible for a younger audience. . . . The author succeeds in weaving together threads of self-acceptance, individuality, what it means to be a friend, and even responsible Internet use. A strong addition to library collections."
—*School Library Journal*

"Tally's transformation and insights in her first-person narrative ring true, as does the rest of the novel: she's surrounded with complex, interesting characters in a realistic plot that nicely captures middle-school experiences and friendships."
—*Booklist*

Praise for

Halfway Normal

★ "Readers will feel with her as Norah struggles with how, when, and to whom she should tell her story—if at all. Dee, whose acknowledgments hint at family experience with childhood cancer, does an exceptional job accurately depicting Norah's

struggles in a way that is translatable to those with varied understanding of illness. . . . A powerful story not only about illness, but about accepting yourself for who you are—no matter the experiences that shaped you."
—*Kirkus Reviews,* starred review

★ "A powerful story about surviving and thriving after serious illness."
—*School Library Journal,* starred review

"The authenticity of Norah's story can be credited to the author's own experiences as the mother of a cancer patient. But this is not a book about cancer; rather, it's about the process of moving forward in its wake. Readers who appreciate well-wrought portrayals of transformative middle-school experiences, such as Rebecca Stead's *Goodbye Stranger* (2015), will find a story in a similar spirit here."
—*Booklist*

"In writing this remarkable novel, Barbara Dee has performed an amazing feat. She has traveled to places you hope you will never have to go and then drawn a lovely, heartbreaking, warm, funny, and ultimately hopeful map of the way back home."
—**Jordan Sonnenblick,** author of
DRUMS, GIRLS, AND DANGEROUS PIE

ALSO BY BARBARA DEE

Maybe He Just Likes You

Halfway Normal

Star-Crossed

Truth or Dare

The (Almost) Perfect Guide to Imperfect Boys

Trauma Queen

This Is Me From Now On

Solving Zoe

Just Another Day in My Insanely Real Life

Everything I Know About You

BARBARA DEE

ALADDIN

NEW YORK   LONDON   TORONTO   SYDNEY   NEW DELHI

ALADDIN

An imprint of Simon & Schuster Children's Publishing Division
1230 Avenue of the Americas, New York, New York 10020
First Aladdin paperback edition October 2019
Text copyright © 2018 by Barbara Dee
Cover illustration copyright © 2018 by Jenna Stempel
Also available in an Aladdin hardcover edition.

For information about special discounts for bulk purchases, please contact
Simon & Schuster Special Sales at 1-866-506-1949 or business@simonandschuster.com.
The Simon & Schuster Speakers Bureau can bring authors to your live event. For more
information or to book an event contact the Simon & Schuster Speakers Bureau
at 1-866-248-3049 or visit our website at www.simonspeakers.com.
Designed by Laura Lyn DiSiena
The text of this book was set in Minion Pro.
Manufactured in the United States of America 0819 OFF
2 4 6 8 10 9 7 5 3 1
The Library of Congress has cataloged the hardcover edition as follows:
Names: Dee, Barbara, author.
Title: Everything I know about you / by Barbara Dee.
Description: First Aladdin hardcover edition. | New York : Aladdin, 2018. |
Summary: "Misfit Tally is forced to room with queen bee Ava on the seventh grade's
extended field trip to Washington, DC, and discovers several surprising things about her
roommate, including the possibility of an eating disorder"—Provided by publisher.
Identifiers: LCCN 2017040921 | ISBN 9781534405073 (hardcover) |
ISBN 9781534405080 (pbk) | ISBN 9781534405097 (eBook)
Subjects: | CYAC: Interpersonal relations—Fiction. | Friendship—Fiction. | School
field trips—Fiction. | Washington (D.C.)—Fiction. | Anorexia nervosa—Fiction.
Classification: LCC PZ7.D35867 Eve 2018 | DDC [Fic]—dc23
LC record available at https://lccn.loc.gov/2017040921

For Lizzy, beautiful inside and out

Boxes

WE GOT TO SCHOOL IN the dark that morning, already fifteen minutes late.

By then, cars were headed in the opposite direction, doggy heads hanging out the passenger windows, horns honking good-bye. Ms. Jordan was standing by the fancy bus, wearing jeans (*she owned jeans?*), checking her clipboard. She looked up; now I could see she was talking to Ava Seeley and her mom, a blond woman dressed head to toe in beige, like she was about to go on a safari.

Suddenly I had the feeling Ava was glaring at me. I mean,

my brain told me she wasn't; we were maybe thirty feet away from her, in a car, and probably she couldn't even see me through the windshield. But she was the head clonegirl of our grade, basically my enemy, so I was always on the lookout for her nasty expressions.

"Gug," I said, my stomach knotting.

"Tally, don't *decide* this will be bad before anything happens," Mom said.

"Yeah, well. Too late."

"Come on, honey, you got this." Mom gave me a pep smile, which usually worked. Although not this time. "Just share the goodies Dad baked you; that'll help with the bus trip. Oh, and here's a present from me."

She handed me a small sandwich bag. Inside were two red things that looked like cap erasers.

"Earplugs," Mom explained. "For the bus. And the room, if Ava's a snorer."

"If she is, she couldn't be louder than Spike." My dog was a champion loud breather, so I was an expert at ignoring snores. Obviously, Mom meant the earplugs for more than snoring.

I stuck the bag in my pants pocket and threw my arms around her. "Thanks, Mom."

She smooched my cheek. "You're welcome, Daughter. Text me when you get there, okay? Tell Spider to text his mom too. And let me help with the bakery boxes."

We stepped out of the car into the sharp, chilly air. It didn't even feel like September, really—although maybe that was because it still seemed liked night. Maybe once we were on the road, and the sun was up, it would feel like a normal fall morning in Eastview.

But not yet. I shivered.

Mom carried two of the boxes, and I carried one, plus my duffel bag. The bus had this huge underneath storage compartment, but by now it was completely crammed with everyone's stuff for the next four days. So we had to wedge my duffel in sideways, probably squishing all the extra cookies Dad had packed.

Then we walked over to Ms. Jordan.

"Good morning, Tally!" Ms. Jordan greeted me too energetically, as if she'd had an extra cup of coffee for breakfast. "I was starting to worry you wouldn't make it. You're Mrs. Martin?" she asked Mom.

Mom caught my eye. Because I'm so much bigger and taller than the rest of my family, people say stuff like this sometimes. Maybe Ms. Jordan didn't mean it as an actual question—*Are you really Tally's mom?*—but it was hard to tell.

"Yes, I am," Mom said, smiling at everyone. Even at Ava, who didn't bother to smile back.

But Ms. Jordan did. "Quite a daughter you have there. Full of character."

Mom nodded. You could tell she was trying to figure out whether that was a compliment.

Meanwhile, Ava's mom was reaching out her hand to shake Mom's, completely ignoring the fact that Mom was holding two bulging bakery boxes. "Good morning. I'm Ellen Seeley," she announced. "I'm the parent chaperone for this trip."

The parent chaperone? But there were three other parents going, I was sure of it.

"Oh yes," Mom said pleasantly. "We've already met, Ellen. How nice of you to volunteer! Tally, could I please give you these boxes? The car is in a no-parking zone, so I really can't stay." Her eyes were begging; she obviously wanted to escape Ellen Seeley.

"Sure," I said, stacking Mom's boxes on top of mine. "You'd better hurry, so you don't get a ticket."

Mom tiptoed to kiss my cheek. "Have fun, sweetheart,

and remember those earplugs," she murmured. "Tune out *whatever* you need to, okay? And don't forget to text." Then she raced off.

Mrs. Seeley turned to talk to Ms. Jordan, as Ava narrowed her eyes at me. "So what's in the boxes?" Ava asked.

"Oh, these?" I said. "Binoculars. Pickaxes. Flashlights. You know, assorted extremely high-tech devices for exploring our nation's capital."

"Huh," Ava said. She never appreciated my sense of humor. "It looks like bakery stuff."

"We're allowed to bring snacks," I informed her. "Not that I *am*."

"Whatever."

"What does *that* mean?"

"It means bring whatever you want, Tally. However *much* you want. I really don't care *what* you do, all right?"

"That's so funny, Ava," I replied. "Because you always act like exactly the opposite."

Now Ava definitely was glaring, and I glared right back at her. She was teeny, maybe ten inches shorter than me, so I had to stoop a bit to make eye contact. But it's hard to stoop while balancing three bakery boxes, so I sort of teetered in her direction.

Finally she said, "Well, you'd better get a seat. You're late, and we're about to leave."

And we know you'd hate to leave me behind, wouldn't you, Ava?

I climbed on board, my heart banging so loudly I was sure you could hear it over the bus engine.

Because here it was. We'd now arrived at the moment I'd been dreading for the past two weeks.

The moment I'd find out if my friends had shown up.

Or if I'd have to do this thing—all three days and four nights—stuck in a room alone with Ava Seeley.

We Hold These Truths

I STOOD AT THE FRONT of the crowded bus, balancing the boxes, scanning the rows. Where were they? Had Sonnet and Spider chickened out, the way I was terrified they would? Especially Spider, who'd texted me at eleven last night: Umm, not so sure about this. . . .

Nono, it will be fun!!!! I'd texted back.

But he'd never answered, which meant I hadn't slept very much, even with Spike's cuddling.

I looked past all the clonegirls in the front rows, then Mr. Gianelli and the chaperones: Mia Gilroy's mom, Althea

Packer's mom, Jamal Melton's dad. Finally I spotted Sonnet waving at me from the second-to-last row.

I breathed.

Then, clutching the boxes with sweaty hands, I made my way down the aisle, past classmates who were either half-asleep or much too perky for five fifteen in the morning.

The way this sort of fancy bus worked was: window, two seats together, aisle, one seat, window. I guess to save the entire row, Sonnet and Spider had split up, with Sonnet sitting by the window in the two-seat part, and Spider across the aisle by himself. So, like usual, my seat was in the middle—next to Sonnet, across the aisle from Spider.

But also right in front of Marco Sarris and Trey Donaldson. Which meant that for the next six and one-quarter hours, there'd be no vacation from Spider's possibly-former-but-I-wasn't-sure-about-this enemies.

Oh, bleep.

"Where *were* you, Tally?" Spider was asking. "Why were you late?" His soft brown eyes were enormous.

"Sorry," I said, handing him the top box. "Dad insisted on making cinnamon buns this morning. And then of course he had to do the icing. You didn't think I'd just forget to *show*, did you?"

I recycled Mom's pep smile for him, but he didn't smile back.

"Nah, I knew you'd make it," Spider admitted. He opened the box. "Whoa, awesome. Your dad rules."

"He definitely does," I said, giving the second box to Sonnet. "These are from the bakery. He made them yesterday, but they're still pretty fresh."

She squealed when she saw the box had giant chocolate chip cookies. My box had some Cinna-mmm muffins and a few blondies. To be honest, the cookies and blondies kind of made me queasy this hour of the morning, but I figured I'd change my mind about them later.

"We can trade," I announced as I settled into my seat. "Plus there's a ton more stuff in my duffel bag. Dad kind of went crazy with the bakery products. I barely had room for my treasure box."

"Wait," Sonnet said. "You brought your treasure box, Tally?" She asked this quietly, like it was a secret between the two of us.

"Yeah, of course. I'd never travel without my treasures. Why would I?"

"I don't know. Ms. Jordan said not to bring precious things on the trip, right?"

"Well, but they're not 'precious things.' Just precious to *me*."

"But what if they get lost or something?"

"That's why I brought the treasure box. So they *won't* get lost."

"I know, but." Sonnet began chewing on her thumbnail. "Maybe they're too precious for this trip."

Sonnet always dressed in such a careful, boring way—all her tops the colors of fall fruit, little gold studs in her ears, nothing in her straight black hair but a red ponytail holder—so probably she didn't understand why I needed my treasures with me. But I knew she thought they were cool, because she said so all the time. She even used that specific word: "cool."

Was Sonnet worried that they wouldn't be safe in a room with Ava? Or was she worried about something else? Either way, it was extremely strange.

I glanced over at Spider. He was fine, just eating a bun and reading one of his space books. I didn't envy a whole lot about him, but the way he could read wherever—in moving vehicles, the noisy cafeteria, dark movie theaters—seemed kind of like a superpower, really. And he didn't even need earplugs.

A jab on my shoulder.

"Hey, Math Girl, your dad *baked* you all of that?" Marco was practically hanging over my seat, salivating like a cartoon wolf.

"Yeah," I said. "He's a baker. So you know, he bakes."

"Cool. You're so lucky."

"Yeah, I know."

"Wish someone in *my* family baked like that."

Obviously, he was waiting for me to offer him something. Well, too bad for him. I didn't forget things so easily. And I didn't feel the need to bribe him. At least, not yet.

Sonnet's cheeks were already bulging with cookie. "Eelikeshoo," she murmured.

"What?" I said.

She chewed and swallowed. Then she leaned over and whispered with chocolate breath: "He likes you."

"Don't be preposterous."

"No, no, I mean it. He asked if you'd be sitting here when he took the seat."

"Well, that was stupid. Of *course* I'd be, if you and Spider were here."

Suddenly Sonnet did a bizarre thing: *She passed her box of cookies to Trey and Marco.* "You should try these; they're amazing," she told them, blushing.

I kicked her in the shin.

She looked at me blankly, so I pulled out my phone and texted her:

Me: Why did you do that?

Her: Why not?

Me: Dad baked for ME to share with MY FRIENDS. They are NOT MY FRIENDS!!!

Her: Well maybe they could be, if we're nice they could be nice back

Me: ARE YOU SERIOUS

Her: yeah Why not

Me: !!!!they bullied Spider!!!!

Her: Well people change, I dunno they seem nice now

I couldn't believe this. The cookies weren't even Sonnet's; I'd just handed them to her for the trip. So what right did she have to pass them to an Evil Nemesis—or to anyone, really?

Finally Ms. Jordan, Ava's mom, and Ava climbed onto the bus. Ms. Jordan said something to the driver, Ava took her seat with Nadia Ramirez and the other clonegirls they hung out with, and *brrmm*, we were off.

We'd barely pulled out of Eastview before these girls

started singing *Hamilton*. Haley Spriggs, of course, was the loudest; she had the best voice, too, so she was Angelica, Ava was Eliza, and Nadia Ramirez was Peggy:

> *We hold these truths to be self-evident*
> *That all men are created equal*

And Sonnet was singing right along with them. Of course, they couldn't hear her all the way in the back of the bus, but the funny thing was how her singing was a decibel too loud, like she was hoping that somehow her voice would carry to their seats, and they'd come racing down the aisle with their arms outstretched: *Ooh, look, our long-lost Schuyler sister!*

A weird question popped into my head: *Does Sonnet wish she was sitting in the front, with the clonegirls, singing along? Maybe she does. And considering how she's rooming with that awful Haley Spriggs—*

Okay, click on a different thought, I ordered myself.

I peeked at Spider, who turned a page in his book. He'd tuned everything out, it seemed. Including me.

And suddenly Ava's voice—high and piercing, surprisingly

strong for such a teeny person—took over the bus, drowning out everything, including the bus engine.

> *Look around, look around,*
> *At how lucky we are to be alive right now—*

I stuck in the earplugs and shut my eyes.

The Ugly Tee

SOMETIMES WHEN YOUR BRAIN HAS nothing better to do, it focuses on weird things, replaying them over and over in an endless loop. And as I half-dozed on that crazy-long bus trip, what I kept replaying in my head was Seventh Grade Spirit Day from a few weeks ago.

It started off with the Handing Out of the Ugly Tee. Which, first of all, was the color of that greenish jellybean with the weird un-candy-like taste, which you can never remember if it's kiwi or sour apple and try to avoid but end up eating before you realize it's lima bean avocado.

Which, second of all, said EASTVIEW MIDDLE SCHOOL ROCKS! And underneath that: SEVENTH GRADE HAS THE SPIRIT! And underneath that: GO BULLDOGS! With a drawing of a slobbering bulldog inside both the *O*s.

"Okay, I'm not wearing that," I informed Ava Seeley, who, along with her clonegirl friend Nadia Ramirez, was handing out tees in front of the auditorium.

"Tally, you *have* to," Ava told me. She was wearing a doll-sized tee that looked shrunk from the dryer. If I had a tee that size, I'd use it as a hankie or something.

"Or what?" I challenged her.

"Or you can't attend the Spirit Day assembly," Nadia said. "And then you won't know anything about the trip."

"I fail to see what wearing that vomitocious tee has to do with the trip."

Nadia rolled her eyes. "Tally, you think the *tee* is ugly, but you're wearing a weird *bat barrette* in your hair—"

I touched the barrette that was keeping my dark, wavy hair out of my eyes. "It's not weird," I said huffily. "It's an actual replica of a baby fruit bat. I got it at a flea market."

"My point exactly," Nadia said.

"Tally, the tees are for seventh grade unity," Ava insisted. "Everyone's wearing them today. Here." She reached into the pile and pulled out a shirt. "Size *large*," she said, shoving it at me.

It was the shove. Also the way she pronounced the word "large," leaning extra hard on the *r* sound: *Larrrrge*. Also the look in her eyes—a judgment. As if large equaled something bad.

I held the tee in front of me, pretending to inspect it. "Wait, that might not be my size," I said. "Are these things unisex?"

"It doesn't matter," Ava said. "It'll definitely fit you, Tally."

For such a teeny girl, she sure had a loud voice. *Well, fine*, I thought. Possibly it *would* fit me. I flipped it inside out and pulled it on over my own SAVE THE SQUIDS tee, backward. "Tally, you can't—" Ava began.

"Sure I can," I said. "Behold."

I marched into the auditorium. Spider and Sonnet were sitting in the third row, on the aisle, and they'd saved me the seat between them. Spider never noticed what I was wearing, even when I came to school in one of my treasures like that necklace I'd made out of soda-can tabs, or the sleeves from Grandma Wendy's fringed suede jacket. So it wasn't surprising that he barely even looked at me as I took the seat.

Sonnet, on the other hand, appreciated my anti-fashion

sense. But she still made a scrunched face at my backward/inside-out tee.

"Um, Tally?" she said. "How come you're—"

"It's a protest," I answered.

"Against what?"

"This T-shirt, obviously. Don't you think it's *preposterous* how they're making us all wear this thing? The color's like moldy guacamole."

"Yeah, Tally," she replied, smiling. "But it's the same color backward and inside out. You haven't solved anything."

I shrugged. "At least now there's no stupid logo on my chest. And no dog spit."

Before Sonnet could respond, the principal, Mr. Barkley, walked up to the microphone and started talking about how the upcoming seventh grade field trip to Washington, DC, was a tradition but also a privilege (which could be taken away, if we misbehaved), how he was sure we were going to have the Best Time Ever, and that we'd never forget the four days and three nights we were soon to spend Maturely and Well-Behavedly in Our Nation's Capital. When he finally finished, he wiped his bald head with a handkerchief and handed the mic to Ms. Jordan, who I had for social studies and also homeroom.

Ms. Jordan was young, enthusiastic, fresh out of teacher school. Everything about her was shiny. Her light brown hair was shiny; her teeth were shiny; her eyes were shiny. All her outfits practically still had tags.

She grinned at us. "Are you all ready for the seventh grade trip?"

Kids screamed.

Apparently, she hadn't expected the screaming. She blushed; she laughed; then she made some *settle down* motions with her hands. When those didn't work, Mr. Barkley snatched the mic back from her and reminded us One More Time about his Expectations for Our Behavior.

People finally shut up. So Mr. Gianelli, the other social studies teacher, started a PowerPoint of all the places we might be visiting (but only if we behaved!). He added that if there was "sufficient interest," he and the other adults on the trip would be "open to other possibilities."

I poked Spider. "We should tell them about the Air and Space Museum."

Spider's eyes lit up. "Yeah." But right away he shook his head. "Nah, they won't want to go."

"Don't say that! It's a really cool place, right? Why wouldn't they?"

He shrugged, like *What's the point?*

Then Ms. Jordan took back the mic.

"As for the hotel," she said. "We'll be staying at the Independence, a place we were extremely lucky to find, because they can accommodate all of us—students, teachers, and chaperones. All of their rooms are doubles, and since one of our goals for this trip is to promote class unity, Mr. Gianelli and I will be assigning roommates. If there's some important information you want to share, please let us hear from you as soon as possible."

Immediately, people started buzzing. *ASSIGNING roommates? No, wait. We're supposed to be with our FRIENDS in the hotel! That's the whole point of this trip, to have FUN! They aren't doing this right! It ISN'T FAIR.*

"I'm not going," Spider blurted.

I turned to him. "Why not? Because of this roommate thing?"

"Yeah." His face had gone pale, and his eyes were round and staring.

Uh-oh. I knew that look.

I turned to Sonnet. "Spider just said he isn't going!"

"Really?" Sonnet leaned across me toward Spider. "Why not, Spider?"

"Why *not*?" I said. "Stuck in a room for four whole days with kids we don't even *like*—"

"We won't be 'stuck in a room'; we'll be touring around," Sonnet reminded me. Then she shrugged. "And, I don't know, it could be sort of interesting."

Sonnet had only moved to town last spring, so she didn't know kids here the way I did. I decided to pretend she hadn't used the word "interesting." Because what *was* "interesting," anyway? It was one of those fiftieth-percentile, neutral words that drove me crazy. I liked words in the tenth percentile. Words that *meant* something, in either direction.

"What if I talked to Ms. Jordan," I said.

Spider shook his head. "It won't make any difference."

"Aww, come on. Don't be so negative, Spider. I'm great at arguing, right? And Ms. Jordan is nice; she'll understand how we are."

Was she? Would she? I sounded more confident than I felt. Sonnet and I both had Ms. Jordan for social studies; we'd only been in school for a week, so I didn't have a whole lot of data to form an impression. All I could say for sure was that our teacher was young, new, and nervous. Spider had Mr. Gianelli, who had a full dark beard, rode a motorcycle to school, and competed in Ping-Pong tournaments. All the kids called him Mr. G, which he seemed to like, and everyone agreed that he was cool (except for Spider, who had his own weird standards for coolness).

So far Ms. Jordan and Mr. Gianelli both seemed decent, the kind of teachers who wouldn't ruin a field trip with scavenger hunts and journals. But would either of them let Spider share a room with two girls, even if they were his best—and only—friends?

I couldn't imagine they would, but what choice did we have? Last year, in sixth grade, Spider was bullied so much he had panic attacks. So someone had to try, and of the three of us, I could tell it had to be me.

Open Mind

I WAITED UNTIL ALMOST EVERYONE had left the auditorium to head for second period. For me that was math, which I hated being late for, but getting this room thing settled was more important.

"Ms. Jordan?" I said. "Can I please talk to you?"

"Oh, sure, Tally," she said brightly, as she gathered her papers. "Are you excited about our trip?"

"Extremely," I said. "Especially about the Washington Monument. Did you know it's the tallest freestanding obelisk in the world? Also the world's tallest stone structure?"

Ms. Jordan beamed at me. "No, actually I didn't. What a cool fact—"

"Yes, and it's exactly five hundred and fifty-five feet, five inches tall. I read it online."

"Wow," said Ms. Jordan.

Now my heart was skittering. "Five is my absolute favorite number, and obelisks are my favorite shape. Well, aside from pentagons, which are also Washington, DC-related, obviously. And of course there's also the Capitol dome, which is pretty great too. If you're into geometry like I am. Um."

Out of the corner of my eye I could see Ava and Nadia, and a bunch of their clonegirl friends, hanging out by the auditorium doors. Maybe they were waiting to talk to Ms. Jordan about rooming stuff too. Whatever they were doing there, I didn't want them listening in on my conversation, so I lowered my voice. "Actually, you said we should tell you important information? About rooming?"

"I did," Ms. Jordan said. "Is there something you wanted to share?"

"Yes! Sonnet, Spider, and I need to be together." It came out fast, without any spaces between the words: *Yes-SonnetSpiderandIneedtobetogether.*

Ms. Jordan blinked at me. "In one room? Oh no, I'm

afraid that's impossible, Tally. First of all, the rooms are all doubles. And second, of course you realize there's no coed rooming."

I suspected she'd say this, so I was ready. "But Spider isn't like that. I mean, obviously he's a *boy*, but we've been best friends forever, and—"

"*No*," she cut in. "That's not something we can accommodate. I'm sorry, Tally."

"Okay, so what if you put Sonnet and me in a double right *next* to Spider's room? That way we could be there for him."

"In case what?"

"In case *anything*."

She looked straight into my eyes. "Is Spider being bullied?"

"No, but." I chewed my lip. "It could happen."

Ms. Jordan paused, not taking her eyes off my face. "And is Sonnet?"

"Not at the moment." When Sonnet had moved to Eastview last year, in the middle of sixth grade, she'd tried out for the spring musical. Only, at the audition, instead of singing *Somewhere over the rainbow / bluebirds fly*, what she sang was *bluebirds die*. As soon as Sonnet realized it, she froze and started panic-giggling. And then Haley

Spriggs, who always got the lead, sent her a card that said *RIP, Bluebirds,* which made Sonnet feel more humiliated, as if that were possible. But I kept telling her how great her voice sounded, which was how we became friends.

Now Ms. Jordan was frowning at me. "Tally, is there anything else you'd like to tell me? Because I'm not really following."

I swallowed. "The thing is, Spider doesn't want me talking behind his back."

"Okay, so would he like to share something himself? He can speak to me, or to Mr. Gianelli. Or perhaps to a guidance counselor—"

"He won't," I said. For the last few months Spider had been seeing an out-of-school therapist named Dr. Spielvogel—a nice woman he liked, and who'd been helping him stay calm lately. But I knew he couldn't handle any more talking, because sometimes he complained about going to weekly sessions. "And now he says he isn't going on the trip," I added.

"Oh. Well, I'm very sorry to hear that, Tally. But you know the trip isn't mandatory. If he'd prefer to stay home—"

"But that's not fair!" I exploded. "Spider shouldn't be forced to stay behind! And if you want my opinion, this whole 'assigning roommates' thing is a terrible idea. Really *terrible*," I repeated, just in case she hadn't heard it the first time.

By then Ms. Jordan's smile looked a lot less shiny. And her makeup looked sweaty, a bit like melted crayons, I thought.

"Well, I'm very sorry you feel that way, Tally," she said. "But this trip is about bonding as a grade, not just about US history. So if you approach it with an open mind—"

But my mind *was* open. Sometimes *too* open, according to some people.

"My mind isn't the problem," I informed her.

She grabbed her tote bag. "Oops, the bell's about to ring for second period. We can talk more later, if you want. And Tally? This is a day about unity, so please fix that tee."

My *tee*? For a second, I didn't get what she was talking about. By the time I processed it, she was hurrying out of the auditorium, as if she wanted to escape.

Math Girl

AVA SEELEY WAS IN MY accelerated math class, even though she wasn't a math person, just the sort of person who was good at taking tests. All sorts of tests, not just math. Everything written in her perfectly even, squarish handwriting. Work all shown, extra credit all done, directions all followed. She even erased without leaving smudges or little eraser droppings.

To me she was the scariest clonegirl in our entire school. Not only because she was all rah-rah, school spirit, but also because she was Miss Perfection: straight As in everything.

Straight golden-brown hair, parted in the middle. Skin with zero freckles, warts, bruises, or zits. Straight fingernails all the same length, polished cotton-candy pink. Every outfit super coordinated and trendy, all hugging her skinny, symmetrical body.

I mean, *geometric shapes* were supposed to be perfectly symmetrical, not *people*. But it was like Ava thought she was a rectangle: no wiggly lines or incongruent angles. And she had to prove it to everyone, all the time. On graph paper.

Plus, she was mean. Not in a playground-bully sort of way, like Trey Donaldson and Marco Sarris, who'd terrorized Spider until I made them stop. More in a quiet, sneaky sort of way, which you didn't notice until it was too late. Even if she didn't say actual mean sentences, I knew she was always judging. Sizing you up with her hazel eyes. In my case, literally sizing.

"Are you okay, Tally?" she asked sweetly as I plopped into my assigned seat next to her.

I grunted. "No."

She smiled. "Maybe your luck would reverse if you turned your tee around."

Had she really just said that? "Ava, why is my tee such an obsession for you?"

"It's not an *obsession*. I just don't want you ruining our celebration."

"You can't possibly be serious."

"Listen, Tally, maybe *you* don't care about Spirit Day, but the rest of us—"

"The rest of you can stuff it," I said.

At that exact moment, our teacher, Mr. Santiago, walked into the room. Without saying hello, he picked up a blue marker and started writing a long problem on the board. Which Ava immediately began copying in her perfectly even, squarish handwriting.

I never raised my hand in math, on principle. "Thirty-six-point-two miles," I announced, a millisecond after Mr. Santiago stopped writing.

He smiled, which for him was a 180-degree line across the bottom third of his face. "Very good, Tally," he said. "Can you explain your answer?"

"Yes, I *can*," I said. "But do I have to?"

"Come on, Math Girl." Marco was laughing as he poked my shoulder. "He means how'd you get that so fast?"

"Neurons," I replied.

Marco blushed.

And I didn't feel one atom of guilt for embarrassing him. After the way he'd treated Spider last year, he deserved it.

Elevator Shaft

THAT NIGHT IT OCCURRED TO me that maybe the problem was, in fact, the T-shirt. Maybe Ms. Jordan had reacted the way she had because she saw me as the Problem Kid, rebelling against something as meaningless as Ugly T-Shirt Day. And maybe if I'd been dressed the official clonegirl way starting that morning at the assembly, she'd have listened more sympathetically. And wouldn't have tried to escape from the auditorium.

So even though it made me crazy to do this, the next morning I put on the Ugly Tee *again*, this time over my

Jellyfish Rescue-thon tee. To this outfit I added a personal touch: Grandma Wendy's ringtail-lemur necklace and a scarf with a banana pattern (*a banana bandanna!*). I took Spike outside to do her dog business; then we came into the kitchen for breakfast.

"Ooh, look at you, Tally, school spirit two days in a row," my big sister, Fiona, teased. She was eating one of Dad's newest muffins, which he called Good Mornin' (no *g* at the end, to sound more casual, I guessed). Mom and Dad owned a bakery in town called Baked Goodies, and they were always bringing home samples and leftovers. For some reason, they always named the muffins: Cinna-mmm, Brantastic, Chocolate Chip off the Old Block, Raisin the Roof.

I poured myself some OJ and took a big muffin with a top that looked like a lumpy pillow. These were always my favorites: the lopsided muffins, the ellipsis-shaped cookies, the brownies that didn't have four right angles. Because who wanted geometrically perfect pastries? In my opinion, geometric perfection was for buildings. And the Washington Monument.

"Yep, that's me," I told my sister. "Miss Eastview Middle School, rockin' the official seventh grade tee. Woo-hoo."

Fiona laughed. "Although I must say, that shade of green is *not* flattering."

I took a bite of sweet, carroty muffin. "Yeah, well, Ava Seeley designed it, and she didn't ask for anyone's input on the color. Or anything else."

"Why am I not surprised?" Fiona asked. She was in tenth grade, but she hadn't forgotten what it's like in middle school. So sometimes I told her things—and not just about Ava.

Suddenly I had a brilliant idea. "Hey, Fiona, are there any extra muffins?"

"Yeah, there's an extra box on top of the fridge. Why? You're not feeding them to Spike, are you?"

"I'm just bringing them to school. For Sonnet and Spider."

Which was true, although indirectly. The muffins wouldn't be a bribe, exactly, just a little teacher gift. Ms. Jordan had had a rough day yesterday, so of course she'd appreciate a little chewy, carroty muffin-ness before homeroom. I mean, who wouldn't, right?

As soon as I got to school, I slipped the banana bandanna in my jeans pocket and knocked on her homeroom door.

"Good morning, Ms. Jordan," I said pleasantly. "Isn't it a lovely day?"

She sipped some coffee from a paper cup. "It's raining, but yes, Tally. I suppose it's lovely."

I waited a second for her coffee to kick in. "Hey, so I brought you something. From my parents' bakery." I placed the open muffin box on her desk.

She gaped. Her first-ever teacher gift, I bet. "Oh, that's so sweet! Thank you so much, Tally! But I already had my breakfast. Maybe I'll save it for a snack later."

"Okay, sure. They're called Good Mornin' muffins, but they're edible whenever, really." I watched her sip more coffee. "So, um, about the room situation. I don't think I explained it very well after the assembly. The thing is, my friends were both bullied last year. Haley Spriggs teased Sonnet a *lot*, and Marco and Trey were both *extremely* mean to Spider."

"Yes, I think I heard something about that," Ms. Jordan said immediately. "But everything's fine now, right? Isn't that what you told me yesterday—no more bullying?"

I nodded. *Why was she asking this question? And why is she making eye contact like this?*

Suddenly I understood about the room assignments.

My stomach dropped down an elevator shaft.

"Oh," I blurted.

"You know, Tally, people change," Ms. Jordan said. "They grow up. Even boys."

"Not all of them!" My voice was too loud, but so what. "Some people *stay* horrible. And you definitely shouldn't be forced to room with them. In a *hotel*!"

"I agree," she said quietly. "Some kids *are* best to avoid. But other kids deserve a second chance, don't you think? Also, don't you think it's important to get out of your comfort zone a little, open yourself up to making new friends—"

"Actually, I'm perfectly comfortable with my comfort zone! That's why it's a *comfort* zone!"

Ms. Jordan did the kind of neutral expression they probably teach you in teacher school. "Well, Tally," she finally said, in a fiftieth-percentile sort of voice, "I can see you're a very caring person."

I still didn't breathe. "Thank you."

"But you're going to have to trust me on this, okay? We've given this a lot of thought; we've had plenty of input from the faculty, including Mr. Barkley, and I'm sure Mr. Gianelli and I can handle anything that comes up. Not that I *expect* anything to. Getting you guys to mix things up socially will be a wonderful way to build class unity. And I feel certain this trip will be a memorable— Oh, hello, girls."

Ava, Nadia, and Haley Spriggs had barged into the classroom. Without saying hello, or even looking at me, or asking if they were interrupting anything, they presented Ms. Jordan with a poster-sized floor plan of the Hotel Independence, which they'd found on the internet and annotated with blue and red Sharpie.

"We know you're doing room assignments for the trip," Ava announced. "And my mom had this great idea. Since the whole third floor of the hotel is shaped like a *T*, if you assign these six rooms in this order—"

Ms. Jordan stared at the names written on the floor plan in Ava's perfect, squarish handwriting. "You did the room assignments yourselves?"

"Only for our friends," Ava said, pretending to sound apologetic. "We knew how crazy it would be fitting everyone into the floor plan. So we thought we'd help make you a chart."

"Like a graphic organizer," Nadia added, using a social studies–type word.

"Whoa," I said. "You're really serious, Ava?"

"About what?" Ava asked innocently. She cocked her head like a tiny bird.

"This floor plan, obviously. You think *you* get to decide—"

"All right, Tally," Ms. Jordan interrupted.

"But this is just *so wrong*, Ms. Jordan!" I exploded. "I can't be with my friends, but Ava gets to assign—"

"No," Ms. Jordan said. "Only teachers do the assigning."

"Wait, at the assembly you said you wanted information from us about rooming," Ava reminded her. "And that's why we thought—"

Ms. Jordan held up both hands. "That's not what I meant, but I guess I should have been more clear. And really, girls, this trip's not about the hotel, and it's not even just about exploring the capital. It's about coming together as a grade: *E pluribus unum*, which is Latin for—"

"'This trip is going to suck'?" Nadia suggested.

"No." Ms. Jordan said, not smiling. "It means 'Out of many, one.' Maybe I'm being too idealistic here, but I really believe you guys *can* become one. For four days, anyway."

I ignored my teacher's speech and snorted at Ava. "All you guys *really* care about is being with your friends. This whole 'class unity' thing is a pile of dog poop."

(I actually used that expression: *pile of dog poop*.)

Ava folded her arms. "Tally, you did *not* just say that."

"Actually, Ava, I did."

"Okay, girls—" Ms. Jordan said.

"No one meant to insult anyone," Haley said. "We were

just trying to make things easier." She seemed upset, but of course, she was an actress, the best one in our grade.

"And maybe we care about our friends because we *have* friends," Nadia added. She flipped her straight dark hair over her shoulder for emphasis.

"Are you saying I don't have friends?" I said. "Because seriously, Nadia, that's just *the most preposterous—*"

"Oh, but Nadia didn't mean that," Haley jumped in.

"Yeah, really? Because to me it sounded like that's *exactly* what she meant."

"*Stop. All of you.*" Ms. Jordan took the floor plan from Ava's hand and dropped it on her desk. "Thank you for the floor plan, girls. I'll look at it later."

"You *will*?" I said. "What for?"

"Tally, all I said was I'll *look* at it. I'm not promising anyone *anything*, okay?"

But Ava beamed. "Oh, you're very welcome, Ms. Jordan," she said.

Folded Pieces of White Paper

RIGHT THEN I GAVE UP. On everything: Rooming with my friends. The trip. Definitely Ms. Jordan. The way I saw it, she was about to do one of two things, both utterly horrible.

Either she'd go along with Ava's bossy, obnoxious floor chart, which would be unfair to everyone who wasn't a clone-girl. (For example, me. And Sonnet. And, of course, Spider.)

Or—and this would be even worse—she'd come up with a room arrangement that basically assigned you to your enemy. Because it was clear Ms. Jordan had some sort of demented newbie-teacher idea about getting people to socialize. Like she thought all you had to do was throw two kids together in a room, chant the magic words "class unity," and, poof, instant friends. No grudges, no bad memories. Why hadn't Mr. Gianelli explained to her that this experiment—or whatever it was—would never work? And also the principal—didn't *he* understand the first thing about middle school?

I went into the girls' bathroom, flipped the spirit tee inside out, and tied the banana bandanna around my neck.

In homeroom, right before dismissal, Ms. Jordan handed out folded pieces of white paper, taped shut. Some kids just stuffed the paper in their pocket to open later, but most opened their papers immediately and groaned. Or shouted something that wasn't a curse (but would've been if we were outside school). Or just rolled their eyes.

I'm not sure why, but I had the feeling I'd need to read my paper in privacy. So I took it to the back of the room.

Talia Martin, your roommate is Ava Seeley.

I swallowed.

Ms. Jordan was watching me with calm, serious eyes.

Across the room, surrounded by her army of clonegirls, Ava Seeley was glaring at me.

And now Sonnet was running over. She looked pale and her eyes were huge. "Tally," she said "Look!"

She gave me her paper. *Sonnet Kobayashi, your roommate is Haley Spriggs.*

"How did she know?" Sonnet murmured. "I mean, why Haley out of everybody?"

I shook my head. "Ms. Jordan said they talked to other teachers. This is all on purpose, to try to make us bond, or something. Don't worry, we don't have to."

"Well, maybe it won't be so bad," Sonnet said in a small voice. She sounded as if she were trying to convince herself but was too smart to fall for it.

All of a sudden, then, I thought of something, and my stomach twisted.

"Come on, we have to find Spider," I muttered, grabbing Sonnet's arm.

We raced out of the room and down the hall to Mr. G's room. Spider was already walking toward us; his face was pale, with the kind of smile that wasn't a smile.

He handed me his room assignment: *Marco Sarris.*

The Dirty Work

SPIDER AND I HAD BEEN best friends since we were toddlers, playing in the sandbox together at Eastview Park. Back then, when he was Caleb, if some kid stole his shovel, he'd turn purple and just start yelling and sobbing, and I'd have to get it back for him. Even if it meant punching the kid.

"Tally, hitting isn't nice," Mom would tell me on the way home from the park. "And anyway, Caleb needs to stand up for himself."

"But he won't," I'd reply.

"He won't because he thinks he doesn't have to. You're doing all the dirty work for him."

I remember thinking about that expression: "dirty work." Yes, we'd been playing in the sandbox, and now we were dirty. So getting his shovel back was *dirty work*.

But I never minded the dirty work of looking after him. My family took care of me, and I took care of Caleb; the world just made sense to me that way. The thing was, I always knew I was adopted, so I always had this idea that love was *choosing* to take care of someone—not just family, but friends, too.

And Caleb needed me: He had no dad, and his mom was not very understanding. All his crying made her constantly scold him and correct him. When we were in fifth grade, some dumb relative told her that if Caleb kept hanging around with me, he'd "turn gay," like you could catch it from being friends with girls. So the next fall she signed him up for Little League, even though he had zero interest in baseball.

The worst part was that I couldn't protect him from very much. The coach, who happened to be Marco's dad, stuck him in left field, and of course it was a disaster. Even if Caleb saw balls coming at him (which he did maybe half the time) his short, skinny arms and legs wouldn't cooperate. He couldn't run fast enough; he'd trip; the ball would go through his legs. Or he'd catch it and drop it. Or he'd catch it, not drop it, but trip as he was throwing it.

Marco and Trey did most of the teasing. They called Caleb "Spider" because he moved "like he's nothing but legs," they said. They even made up a Spider dance, which consisted of flailing their arms and legs like one of those inflatable tube guys you see outside car dealerships, and then falling facedown on the outfield grass.

Soon the whole team was doing the Spider dance.

And did Marco's dad stop them? No.

One day they teased Caleb so much, he had a panic attack right out there on the field, in front of everyone. I wasn't at the game, because I hated baseball even more than Caleb did. But I found out about it the next day at school, when all the kids were talking about how he basically collapsed in the batter's box and couldn't catch his breath. *An asthma attack,* people called it. But if there was a difference between that and a panic attack, I didn't know what it was.

By sixth grade, I was already five foot eight, tall as a

grown-up. Mom told me I was "big-boned," but I was muscly, too, with a squishy belly and a big butt. When I marched over to Marco and Trey and told them to quit it with the Spider dance, they immediately turned on *me*, calling me Super-Size and Big Bird. ("Yeah, I'm big, you subatomic particles," I sneered back at them.) Then they started making spiders out of pipe cleaners, dropping them down Caleb's back, and on his head, and also on his desk and on his lunch tray. Sometimes they even caught real spiders and used them instead. Caleb had this general bug phobia, so whenever he discovered these (mostly dead) spider "gifts," his face would turn white and he'd start gasping and wheezing.

"Ooh, spiders, I'm such a scared wittle girl—where's my big stwong Tallyguard?" Trey said in this cartoon falsetto.

I loomed and glared, but it didn't work. And I knew that if I didn't take some kind of forceful action, the next time Caleb had baseball practice could end up even worse.

So I punched Trey in the mouth.

Mr. Barkley gave me a two-day suspension, but I didn't care. The bullying stopped, and Marco even apologized, for Trey and for himself.

"It won't happen again," he told me. "I promise."

"Why should I believe you?" I growled.

Marco looked right at me, and for the first time I noticed that his eyes were olive green, and that he had thick black eyelashes.

"Because I'm not a liar," he said quietly.

Which struck me as a funny thing to say. I mean, if you're a bully.

In the middle of sixth grade, Marco got put in accelerated math somehow, so of course he realized it was my subject. That's when he started calling me Math Girl. And I decided to let him, because math was what mattered to me, who I actually *was*. The size thing always felt kind of alien, in a funny way—like I had nothing to do with it; it was just my body. My size had more to do with my biological mother, Marisa, a person I'd never even met. And really, no matter how you looked at it, Math Girl was a compliment. It meant I was smart.

That was also when I decided to start calling my best friend "Spider." Over the summer we'd found out that we'd be in separate classes for seventh grade, and I was worried about how he'd be without me. So I decided Caleb needed a new identity.

"Tally, are you crazy?" he protested. "That's an insult!"

"It doesn't have to be," I told him. "Just think about it,

okay? Spiderwebs *look* weak, but they're incredibly strong! And spider bites are painful. Plus, think of Spider-Man. I'll call you Spider in recognition of your *powers*."

He made a sound like *pfft*. "My what?"

"Come on," I said, poking him. "If you want Spider to stop being a negative, just turn it into a positive!"

"You mean by making it my *name*?"

I sighed. Sometimes he could be really stubborn.

"Listen, Caleb, I can't do everything for you, you know," I said. "You have to do *some* dirty work for yourself, all right?"

He thought about it. "Yeah, all right," he finally said. "Go ahead. Call me Spider."

That's how much he trusted me. And so far, the first week of seventh grade, it seemed to be working. No one, not even Marco and Trey, was bothering him, at least not in front of me. Basically, he'd become invisible, and that's not the worst thing, if you've been bullied.

But I knew how easily the bullying could happen again, especially on this trip. *Especially* if Spider was rooming with Marco—who was one iota better than Trey, although really, that wasn't saying much.

Clonegirl

THAT NIGHT AT DINNER, I told my parents about Ms. Jordan's Evil Room Assignments, how she'd deliberately put me with Ava, Sonnet with Haley, and, worst of all, Spider with Marco.

"Seriously, Mom, you should complain to the principal," Fiona said. "Teachers aren't supposed to behave like this."

"Yes, maybe I should," Mom said. I could see she was thinking out loud. "Although Ms. Jordan is a new teacher, so complaining to the principal is a very big deal. It's sort of like she's on probation this year. Maybe we should try to give her a chance."

"But Ava Seeley is *horrible*," Fiona said, catching my eye. "You don't know, Mom."

"No, but I've met her mother." Mom smiled. You could tell she had an opinion she wasn't sharing. Except that by not sharing it, she was sharing it, really. "She started that business where she criticizes your clothes."

"She *what*?" I shouted. "What kind of a business is *that*?"

Mom laughed. "Ellen's sort of a wardrobe consultant, I think. Or a professional woman's life coach–type person. Something one-on-one where she comes to your house, goes through your closets, and gives you advice about how to look. Mostly for business, I think. But anyway, Tally, what's wrong with Ava?"

"Everything," I declared. "She's bossy, she's secretly mean, she's stuck up, she thinks she's perfect, she dresses like a clonegirl—"

"A what?"

"Super fashionable, but exactly the same as everyone else. No originality, no personality. Like it's all been dictated to her from TV and these dumb fashion magazines she's always reading. And if you *don't* dress like that, she decides you're weird. Also, she makes fun of my size," I added.

At that, everyone stopped eating and looked at me. Because I'm adopted, I don't look like the rest of the family. We all have dark hair and tan skin, but the difference is they're small. *Small-boned,* Mom calls it, as if they're all birds. And they're sensitive about my size. I mean, about how people react to my size.

"She makes fun of you?" Dad asked. "What does she say?"

"Nothing specific," I admitted. "But she always looks at me a certain way, like she thinks I'm big just to personally annoy her or something. She always makes these snide comments about how I dress. And when she gave me the tee, she said it was a large. Like this: *Larrrrge.*"

"Hmm," Mom said. "Tally, have you tried sharing how you feel with Ms. Jordan?"

"A million times!" I said. "I even brought her muffins! Now she's sick of me and refuses to discuss it."

Mom and Dad exchanged glances. It was like their brains were having a private conversation.

"Well," Dad finally said. "It looks to me like there are three options here, Tally. One, you stay home."

"Dad, that's unacceptable!" Fiona shouted. "Let Ava stay home! Why should Tally have to?"

"Yeah," I said, chomping on a carrot stick. "You only get one big seventh grade trip."

"Two," Dad continued, "Mom and I complain to the principal."

I shook my head. "It won't make any difference. Ms. Jordan said he's all for it."

Which was true. But I was also thinking about how I was still in semi-trouble with Mr. Barkley for wearing a red fedora in school last week, even after he'd told me to take it off. Possibly I was in trouble for other fashion crimes too, and I knew he was always waiting for me to punch some-one else on Spider's behalf. So I wasn't super eager for any parent-principal interaction.

"Okay, three," Dad said. "You go on the trip and share a room with Ava at night, when you're asleep and won't even notice her, and you spend the daytime touring Washington and hanging out with your friends."

"I know which option *I'd* pick," Mom said. "But it's your choice, sweetheart."

My family looked at me, waiting for my answer. I could tell they wanted me to pick option three, but I knew they'd support me whatever I decided. That was how they were, really, about everything. The total opposite of Spider's mom.

I sighed. "Fine. I pick three. But it still sucks."

"Yes, it does." Mom kissed my cheek. "But you know what, Talia Martin? You got this."

The Spy Game

THE BUS TRIP WAS ENDLESS—a million hours of phone YouTube, staring out the window at the boring highway, eating cookies, staring at the back of Jamal Melton's head, listening to Sonnet's iPod, dozing, ignoring the bus video (*Moana*, which I'd already seen like ten times), trying desperately to ignore Haley and her friends singing *Hamilton* in the front of the bus. And of course trying to ignore Mrs. Seeley, who kept walking down the aisle "to stretch her legs," she told everybody, but I had the feeling she was snooping.

For almost the entire trip, Spider kept reading. It

would've been understandable if he read normal books about kids who discovered a parallel universe of brain-eating slime monsters (for example), but all he ever read was boring nonfiction about his top five subjects: dinosaurs, ancient weaponry, World War II, early aircraft, and space. And even though I wished he'd take a break sometimes to chat, or to play cards with me or something, I was glad to see him ignoring Marco and Trey—not acting jumpy in the slightest, even though they were sitting right behind me. This was new, and to be honest, I didn't know what to think about it. Of course, Marco and Trey were ignoring *him*, the way they'd been doing lately. But would this back-and-forth ignoring continue when Spider was alone in the hotel room with Marco? I wasn't going to bet on it.

At ten forty-five we stopped for snacks, but by then I was so full of Baked Goodies that I just walked around the outside of the bus a few times, texting Fiona.

Me: Hey, how's Spike?

Fiona: You're not going to ask how *I* am?

Me: Yeah, yeah. First tell me about Spike. Did you take her out for bathroom before school? Feed her? Give her water?

Fiona: Affirmative X3. What's going on with Ava??

Me: Nothing. We're stiiiiiiill on the road.

Fiona: Well, if she tries anything evil, say your big sistah is coming after her. ;) And report back to me! I wanna hear *all* the juicy details!!

Those two words—"juicy details"—gave me an idea. A brilliant way to get through the next four days and three nights.

I found Spider and Sonnet by the rest-stop water fountains and motioned them over to this wall where you could get maps.

"Hey, you know what'd make this trip super fun?" I said in my Enthusiastic Voice. "What if we all spied on our roommates, and then reported back to each other?"

"*Spied?*" Spider frowned. "What do you mean by that, exactly?"

"Just noticing little secrets they have, stuff you'd know only by living with a person. Like if they pick their nose, or they sleepwalk. Or if they use some kind of weird deodorant. *Juicy details*," I added.

"I'm not sure," Sonnet said slowly. "Honestly, I don't think Haley *has* 'little secrets.' And anyway, this sounds like the kind of thing *you* do, Tally. Not me."

"Yeah," Spider said, looking over his shoulder to make sure no one was listening. Which, obviously, they weren't.

"And even if Marco does have some kind of secret, what's the point of finding it out? He's been okay with me lately; I don't want to start a fight."

"Of course not," I agreed. "But this isn't about fighting; it's about *knowing* things. And knowledge is power, right?"

Spider sighed. "Listen, Tally. If I have to share a room with Marco, I don't want to be dealing with him any more than I have to. I mean, it's bad enough we'll be breathing the same oxygen."

"Oh, but you're missing the point," I argued. "Spying doesn't mean you have to talk to him or anything! Come on, it'll be fun! And when else will we get a chance like this?"

They both sort of shrugged, so I figured I'd won the argument. Maybe. And if I hadn't convinced them, I told myself, I'd just do the spying on my own.

Finally, two hours later, we arrived at the Hotel Independence. While Mr. G, Mia's mom, and Jamal's dad took care of removing everyone's luggage from the bus, Ms. Jordan, Mrs. Seeley, and Mrs. Packer led us into the hotel lobby—a red, white, and blue food court–shaped space that looked like American Revolution World, with little blacksmith shops and silversmith shops and a candle-making stand. There was a restaurant called the Thomas Jefferson, a tavern called the Ben Franklin, and a coffee bar called the Patrick Henry. A skinny guy in a blue vest and knickers was standing in the corner by a big potted fern, playing a piccolo.

"Omigod, Tally!" Sonnet pointed to a woman behind the registration desk, who was wearing a bonnet. A *bonnet*. Also black hipster glasses, which clashed with the rest of the outfit in a way I appreciated.

"Whoa," I said. "I've never seen anyone wearing an actual bonnet!"

"Maybe she's just having a bad hair day," Sonnet said, giggling.

The woman stepped away from the desk. Now you could see she had on a long blue dress with a full white apron.

I clutched Sonnet's arm, ecstatic. "Sonnet, she's wearing an *entire costume!*"

"I know! Promise you won't dress like that too, okay?" Sonnet said.

I checked; Sonnet was smiling. But it was still a weird thing to say. Did she think I was nuts or something? Who would dress that way in real life?

"Good afternoon, I'm Roy. You're the doctors?" A man in a long red coat and white knee socks was taking off a three-cornered hat as he bowed at Ms. Jordan. When he stood I could see that he had a silver stud in one ear and a snake tattoo on his left hand.

Everyone started giggling and buzzing.

Ms. Jordan smiled. "Oh no, we're not *doctors*. These are seventh graders—"

"We're all booked out," Roy interrupted. "To a group of *doctors*. Sorry, ma'am."

"No, wait!" Ms. Jordan paled. "We have a reservation!"

"Are you sure it's for *this* hotel? There are tons of others—" He waved his snake hand at the revolving door.

"I'm positive. At least I think so." Ms. Jordan frantically scrolled through her phone. "I swear, I couldn't possibly have deleted—okay, found it: Hotel Independence reservation confirmation, dated a month ago. See?"

Roy squinted at her phone. "Yeah, well, there's been a mistake, clearly. Because we're expecting *doctors*."

"Well, what are we supposed to do?" Ms. Jordan's voice squeaked.

"Uh-oh," Spider murmured.

"Best field trip ever," Marco announced. "Totally worth the bus ride!"

"Not funny, Marco," I said.

"No, I'm serious! This place is awesome! Check out those old-timey elevators!"

I looked. Above the elevators were arrows pointing at half moons of numbers. Cool. But not American Revolution-y.

Mrs. Seeley marched over to Ms. Jordan's side. "Excuse me, Mr. . . . ?"

"Just Roy. We don't give out last names."

"Well, I do. I'm Ellen Seeley," she said, extending her hand the way she'd done with Mom. "All right, *Roy*, it's obvious that *you've* made the mistake. Or someone on your staff has. But it certainly wasn't *us*, since *we* have a confirmation."

"Yeah, well." He sighed. "Just because a confirmation is in the system doesn't mean—hey, um, would you excuse me a moment?" He hurried off to whisper to the bonnet-and-hipster-glasses woman behind the registration desk.

Mrs. Seeley followed him.

"Is there a problem, Roy?" she asked in a loud voice. "Because if there is, I'd like to speak directly to the manager."

"Please be patient, ma'am," Roy said, as we all crowded around the registration desk.

"I'm afraid patience is out of the question," Mrs. Seeley

boomed. "We have forty-six exhausted and hungry middle schoolers—"

"*Middle* school?" Hipster Bonnet looked up from her monitor.

"Yes. And we've just driven all the way from Eastview—"

She stared at her monitor. Then she stared at us. "Are you . . . Eastview *Middle* School?"

"Ooh, yeah," Nadia called out, waving invisible pompoms. "We got the spirit! Woo!"

Roy's face relaxed. "Well, that explains it. The system had you down as Eastview *Medical* School. Which is why we were expecting doctors. Or doctor-students, whatever you call them. If we'd known you were a bunch of *kids*—"

"Yes?" Mrs. Seeley asked threateningly. "You'd have what?"

"We don't normally accept reservations from middle schools, but never mind." Roy forced a smile. "You're all on the second and third floors. Which we call Lexington and Concord."

"Aren't Lexington and Concord in Massachusetts, not Washington, DC?" Spider asked.

Sonnet giggled. I saw Haley Spriggs flash her a smile. *What was that about?*

Roy shrugged. "Hey, man, I just work here, okay?"

"The floors are all named after Revolutionary War battles," Hipster Bonnet explained, typing. "Fourth floor is Saratoga, fifth is Yorktown, sixth is Princeton. The main floor, where all the shops and restaurants are, is called Bunker Hill. The gym and the pool are on the lower level, which is called Trenton, and are open twenty-four/seven."

"Hey, pool party!" Trey shouted.

"Not a chance, Trey," Ms. Jordan said, her face a human color again. "All right, listen up. We'll be handing out key cards to your rooms. Girls are on the second—I mean, Lexington—floor, boys are all on Concord, and there's no visiting between floors."

Kids groaned.

"Why can't we va-sat?" Sydney Brunner asked, pouting. She had that snotty way of talking; she called herself Sad-nay. "Ms. Jor-dann, that isn't fair."

Ms. Jordan just shook her head. "Don't worry, you'll have plenty of time to socialize. For now, just relax, wash up, communicate with home. At two thirty we'll meet here in the lobby—with your Eastview spirit tees on, please—take a stroll on the National Mall, and then have dinner. Okay?"

"Sounds great," said Mr. G, who was just then showing

up at the desk with carts heaped with luggage. "But first, claim your belongings, people."

As everyone grabbed their stuff, I heard Mrs. Seeley say to Ms. Jordan, "Dear, I hope you don't mind me saying this, but as a young woman, you need to speak a little more forcefully to the hotel staff, or they'll never take you seriously. It's a life skill I'd be happy to teach you sometime."

Ms. Jordan pressed her lips together as if she wanted to stop words from flying out.

I glanced at Ava, who was rubbing her shoe on the carpeting in little circles.

Treasures

AVA AND I WERE IN room 206, which meant on the second floor. But you had to call it Lexington, apparently, so our room was Lexington 06. Sonnet and Haley were down the hall, in Lexington 14, and Spider was up on the third floor—Concord 22.

The weird thing was how Mrs. Seeley followed Ava and me into Lexington 06. Right away she unzipped Ava's luggage and started hanging up her stuff in the closet, smoothing the fabric with her hand, while Ava leaned back against the pillows, reading her fashion magazines. "Tally, dear, let me know if we're taking up too much closet space," Mrs. Seeley called over her shoulder.

"No, it's fine," I said. "I'm really not a hanger person. I mostly just dump my stuff wherever."

"Well, you really should learn the art of hanging up. I can teach you if you like."

"That's okay, Mrs. Seeley. I prefer the art of dumping."

Ava narrowed her eyes at me. "Aren't you going to unpack?"

Sure. As soon as your mom leaves the room. "In a minute," I said. "I just want to rest a bit first." I did a snow angel on my bed over the comforter, which had a pattern of pale green Revolutionary War battle scenes. Guys with muskets. *The British are coming!* Not very sleep-inducing, I thought.

"So, Tally," Mrs. Seeley said, as she continued hanging. "I'm guessing your dad is a large man?"

"My dad?" I sat up.

"Yes, your mom is so petite, so I thought—"

"No, Dad is petite too. Although 'petite' is probably not the right word. *Is* there a word for a short male person?"

Mrs. Seeley smiled as she zipped Ava's hoodie onto a hanger. "Good question. I never thought of that before. So who do *you* take after?"

"You mean physically? No clue. I'm adopted."

She froze. "Oh! I'm so sorry! It's really none of my—"

"No, I don't mind. Actually, I'm *happy* I'm adopted."

"Yes, and you should be! Your adoptive mom seems lovely!"

"She's not my 'adoptive mom.' She's just my mom."

"Of course! I just meant as opposed to the *other woman*—"

"You mean my bio-mom? Her name is Marisa. I haven't met her yet, but I bet she's a lovely person too."

"Oh, I'm sure!" Mrs. Seeley pretended to focus on hanging up one of Ava's jackets, but I could see how this conversation had her flustered.

The truth was, I didn't know very much about Marisa—I had a photo of her from before I was born, taken on a beach with a bunch of people who looked like they were having a party. Marisa's hair was dark and long; she was sitting behind someone, so I couldn't see her size too well, but she seemed pretty tall. (I mean, *probably*; it's hard to tell when a person is sitting.) She'd written me a few cards and letters when I was a baby, but she stopped after my second birthday. Which had nothing to do with *me*, my parents said. And for all I knew, Marisa was, in fact, a lovely person, and maybe there was a perfectly logical reason why she'd stopped communicating, but I couldn't imagine what it was. So even though I loved my family more than anything, sometimes I wondered about Marisa.

And now, to change the subject, Mrs. Seeley asked what my mom did.

"You mean what's her job?" I said. "She and dad have a bakery."

"Oh, yes, I forgot! How nice. I bet they bring home yummy treats *all the time*. It must be so difficult for you to resist—"

"Mom," Ava said, yawning. "I'm really tired."

Mrs. Seeley smiled brightly. "All right, you girls rest now. See you in the lobby at two thirty. I'm down the hall in room 18 if you need anything, Ava." She blew Ava a kiss, grabbed her own bulging red leather suitcase, and left the room.

"Sorry Mom was being nosy," Ava said as she picked a small yellow notebook off her night table, opened it in her lap, and wrote something quickly.

"That's okay," I replied.

"It's just the way she does her job. She talks to people everywhere we go. And she asks a lot of questions."

"Well, I bet she's very successful."

"Oh, she is," Ava said proudly. "She has a million clients, and a waiting list. But she's always looking for more. She says that's how you build a business."

Did Mom and Dad know this? I wondered as I unzipped my duffel bag. They never talked about "building" their bakery business—they just did it every day. And if people liked what Dad baked, they came back for more. Maybe business was different when it came to food. Especially bakery food, which was just about making people happy.

I took out my treasure box and put it on the table next to my bed. Mostly what was in it used to be Grandma Wendy's: the bicycle-chain bracelet, a pair of green cat's-eye glasses with rhinestones forming the Big Dipper, this possibly antique pocket watch with the hands missing. Some of the other things were from the flea markets she'd taken me to, like the ringtail-lemur necklace, the mustache-shaped earrings, and the purple newsboy cap. And maybe I'd wear this stuff on the trip, or maybe I wouldn't, but it made me feel good to have it by the bed. Whatever Sonnet thought about it, anyway.

Then I inspected the Baked Goodies in my duffel: The muffins were a bit smashed, but the brownies and blondies had survived intact.

Ava watched as I lined them up on my night table. "What's all that food?" she asked.

"From my parents' bakery. You want something?" After the way she'd reacted to the bakery boxes at the bus, I'd vowed not to share anything with her. But the question just blurted itself out, I guess.

She shook her head. "No thank you. I don't eat that stuff."

"Seriously? How come?"

"I just don't."

"That's not an answer."

"Fine," Ava said, sighing. "Too many carbs, all right?"

I burst out laughing.

"You think that's funny?" she said.

"Well, yeah. What do you care about carbs, Ava? You're such a stick."

Her mouth twisted. "If I'm thin it's because I pay attention to what I eat. If I ate all that stuff like you do, I'd be fat."

I raised my eyebrows. "Whoa. Are you saying I'm fat?"

"No. I'm saying *I'd* be fat. Tally, why do you always have to turn everything into a fight?" She tossed her yellow notebook onto her pillow and stomped into the bathroom, slamming the door.

Okay, so this was going super well.

I nibbled a bit of muffin, then texted Mom: Hey, I'm here. No answer, so I stood up and stretched. I watched myself in the full-length mirror opposite my bed: one, two, three, streeeetch. Then I watched myself do seven jumping jacks, how my boobs and belly had their own separate timing. *It would be nice to have a mirror this size in my bedroom,* I thought, *so I could see how it looks when I'm dancing.* Not that it would matter—I'd still dance, whatever I looked like. Even if my body jiggled at different speeds. Which it did, apparently. Huh.

And then, before I'd completely caught my breath, I did something I can't explain: I went over to Ava's pillow to peek at her yellow notebook. On a page with today's date, she'd written in her perfect, squarish handwriting, but tinier than normal:

65

200?

12

approx 150

25

The toilet was flushing, so I shut the notebook, returned it to her pillow, and started dumping things from my duffel bag into the chest of drawers Ava wasn't using.

Ava walked back into the room. "This hotel is weird," she announced. "All the soap has pictures of George Washington."

"Fighter of tyranny and germs!"

She didn't laugh. She just perched on her bed and reached for the room phone. "Hello," she said loudly, in a grown-up-sounding phone voice. "This is Lexington zero six. Who do I speak to about getting a bathroom scale, please?"

It was a strange question, but what I noticed mostly was how her voice sounded just like her mom's. Maybe one day Mrs. Seeley had sat her down in the kitchen and said: *Okay, Ava, this is how you speak to the guy at the front desk.* Or maybe Ava heard her mom's voice so much she didn't even realize she was imitating her.

Then I wondered if I sounded like my mom too. If I did, it wasn't because she *taught* me to sound like her.

Although maybe you picked up stuff from your mom without even knowing it.

Pirate Band-Aids

TEN MINUTES LATER, SONNET TEXTED to ask if I had an extra toothbrush. If anyone else had asked such a dumb question, I'd have texted back: Who carries around extra toothbrushes??? But it was Sonnet, and I thought she was probably freaking about rooming with Haley Spriggs. So I suggested we meet in the lobby (Boston Harbor, or whatever it was called) and check out Ye Olde Apothecary Shoppe, or whatever dumb name they gave it. I texted Spider to come meet us there too, so I could check in with him, see how he was doing with Marco.

I met Sonnet at the toothpaste shelf, which was also the first-aid shelf. Immediately I fell madly in love with a box of pirate Band-Aids.

"Must have," I announced.

"What for?" Sonnet asked over her shoulder as she examined a toothbrush.

"Are you *serious*? Band-Aids with skulls and crossbones? This is the best thing ever. Not very colonial-themed, *but*."

"Well, they did have pirates in those days, right?" Sonnet walked over to me and said in a low voice: "Oh. So I wanted to tell you: I noticed something."

"About what?"

"Haley. You know, for that game we're playing."

"Right." I acted all casual, like *Oh, yeah, of* course *we're playing the spying-on-roommates game!* But in reality I was surprised, because when I'd suggested it to Sonnet, she hadn't seemed all that enthusiastic. "What did you find out?"

"Haley brought a stuffed pink moose to the hotel. Named Peanut."

"Omigod, really?" I squealed. "Like, to sleep with?"

Sonnet made a *shhh* finger. "I think so. I'll let you know."

"That's awesome. Well, nice work, Agent Sonnet."

I was so relieved, I almost gave her a hug. *It was stupid of me to doubt her on the bus, wondering if she'd rather be with Haley and all the clonegirls. Sonnet is a true friend! Also a great spy!*

"What about Ava?" she asked as she checked out the lip glosses.

"You mean spy-wise?" I thought for a second. "Well, her mom hangs up all her clothes for her. And she doesn't eat sweets."

Sonnet frowned. "Really? How come?"

"Too snobby for sugar, I guess. Also, she has a notebook full of dates and numbers."

"Phone numbers?"

"Just number numbers. Random, apparently. Speaking of which." I took out my phone and dialed Spider. He didn't answer, so I texted him: Hey sup, SpiderMan?

I waited. No answer.

Sonnet and I went to pay. The cashier was this pimply guy with a ponytail and a vest with a mustard stain. He had a name button: MIKEL. "Class trip?" he asked us.

"Yep," I said, as I took my change.

"Where from?"

"Greenland. Land of ice and sardines."

Sonnet started giggling behind her hand.

"Huh. Welcome to our nation's capital." He said the line like he was programmed by the hotel.

"So, Mikel, what's your recommendation for must-do activities?"

He thought, as if no one had ever asked him this before. "The regular tourist stuff, I guess. The Air and Space Museum is pretty cool. And the National Zoo."

"Ooh, does the zoo have seals? Seals eat more sardines than humans do, you know."

"Yeah?" He looked unsure.

"Yes, in Greenland seals are considered gods. Demigods, technically."

Sonnet yanked on my shirt.

"Well, Mikel, nice chatting with you," I said.

When we were one step outside the Apothecary Shoppe, Sonnet squealed: *"Sardines?"*

I grinned. "Yeah, I know, but I just felt sorry for that guy. Probably no one ever talks to him, and there he is all day long in a stupid outfit, dripping mustard on himself."

"Well, it's his job," Sonnet argued. "What are you going to do with those Band-Aids?"

"Not sure yet. I need to ponder."

"Maybe you should save them."

"For what?"

"I don't know. Sometime when you have a paper cut."

The way she avoided my eyes, I could tell she was embarrassed. Was this more of what she'd said on the bus—how maybe I should have left my treasure box home? And not to keep my precious things safe from Ava—to keep me from wearing them. In public. I'd only met Sonnet about six months ago. Maybe I didn't know her very well after all.

"Well, I'm absolutely sure I need these Band-Aids," I informed her. Then I texted Spider again. Still no answer. What was going on up on Concord?

"You know, we really should make sure Spider's okay," I said.

Sonnet blinked. "Why wouldn't he be?"

Did she really not get this? "Sonnet, he's not answering his phone, and he *always* answers when it's me. Plus, he's rooming with *Marco*, remember?"

"Well, Marco was acting pretty nice on the bus. Can I ask you a question, Tally? Do you think he's cute?"

"You mean Marco?"

Sonnet nodded.

"Maybe a little," I admitted, thinking about his green eyes, and also those eyelashes. Also, his wavy brown hair that needed a haircut. "But it's totally irrelevant."

"Why?"

"Sonnet, don't you get this? He and Trey *bullied Spider*—"

"Okay, but that was last year, right? Don't you think they've outgrown it? And that maybe Spider can handle them on his own?"

I thought about the way Spider had ignored them on the bus for over six hours. That *was* pretty impressive, I had to admit. Maybe he'd learned some zoning-out tricks from Dr. Spielvogel.

"No offense, Tally," Sonnet was saying, "but sometimes I think you treat Spider like a baby. And he's really *not* one, you know?"

She took a tube of lip gloss out of her bag. I'd been so busy chatting with Mikel that I hadn't noticed she'd bought the lip gloss, and now she was smearing her lips the color of overripe watermelon.

"Well, I just want to see him for a second," I announced.

"But you can't, anyway," Sonnet pointed out. "We're not allowed on the third floor."

"I'll be invisible. Don't come if you don't want to."

Sonnet gave a long, exasperated sigh. It made my stomach knot up, but I didn't say anything.

We walked across the lobby to the elevator. I pushed three and Sonnet pushed two.

"This place is ridiculous," I said. "If they make you *say* Concord, they should put Concord on the elevator button, not three!"

"Yeah," Sonnet said. She sighed again. "All right, fine. I'll come with you."

"You totally don't have to."

"I know." She rolled her eyes like Nadia. "But let's just be fast, Tally, okay?"

The doors opened on two, then closed. On three, as soon as we stepped out of the elevator, there was Mr. G.

"Hey, wrong floor," he said, smiling. "Girls are on two, remember?"

"Oops," Sonnet said. She'd turned pink, of course. "We were thinking, 'Wait, is Lexington two or three?' and it's really hard to keep straight, so—"

"But as long as we're here, can we say hi to Spider?" I cut in.

Mr. G frowned. "Tally, come on, you heard the rule. No socializing between the floors."

"I know, but—"

At the end of the hallway, a door opened. Derrick Chen

and Nick Burrell came crashing out, following a Nerf ball, laughing their dumb heads off.

"Hey, guys, hotel behavior," Mr. G called out.

"Sorry," Derrick said. They stared at us, ran back into their room with the ball, and slammed the door.

"Mr. G, I just want to make sure Spider's okay," I murmured. "He's rooming with someone he despises. And who despises him back."

"That's a little harsh, isn't it, Tally? I'm sure he'll be fine."

"Yes, but what if . . ." I couldn't finish the sentence. What if *what*? Marco did the Spider dance? Dumped bugs in Spider's bed?

Even though I'd spent practically my whole life protecting my friend from bullies and shovel thieves, I really *didn't* believe Marco was capable of those things anymore. Not the Marco who'd apologized for Trey's obnoxious behavior. Who called me Math Girl in a not-insulting way. And who'd been so interested in Dad's baking a few hours ago. I mean, to be truthful, the worst thing I could say about Marco lately was that he ignored Spider.

But Spider was still Spider. And you just never knew how he'd react to things when he was stressed. Even if he *was* seeing Dr. Spielvogel.

Mr. G made eye contact, the kind that teachers use when they really, really want you to shut up. "Tally, I personally give you my word. I'm right next door to their room, so if anything's going on, I'll be the first to hear it. Although I'm sure nothing will. Okay?"

I nodded, because basically I had no choice.

"Good," Mr. G said, checking his watch. "We're all meeting in the lobby in fifteen minutes. Why don't you girls go put on your spirit tees, so when we venture out, we can look like a unified group?"

"Sure," Sonnet said quickly. I could see she was relieved to escape.

"Well, we can definitely try to *look* that way," I said.

Body Type

WHEN I GOT BACK TO the room, Nadia was sitting on my bed. She was on her phone, typing, and she didn't even bother to look up at me.

"Hey, Tally," she said, still typing. "Ava's in the shower."

"Okay," I said. Not that I'd asked.

She finally looked up. "Yeah, she asked me to stay in case they delivered something."

"In case who did?"

"Hotel people. She'd asked them for a scale?"

"Right," I said. "She did."

"I don't know why she needs one. She's like a tooth-pick." Nadia flipped her hair over her shoulder. "So here's a question for you: Why *exactly* are you wearing suspenders?"

"Oh, these?" I looked at my chest. "Yeah, I found these at a tag sale. Aren't they awesome?"

"'Awesome' is not the word. Also, they're orange."

"They look orange to you? To me they're rust. Burnt sienna, possibly."

"Well, they're hideous, whatever you call them. And they do *not* go with those purple pants. Not that anything *does*. But I'm guessing you know that." Nadia yawned, stretching her arms and legs. Finally she stood. "All right, *you* can wait for Ava's scale. I'm going back to my room to change."

"Mr. G said we're supposed to wear our T-shirts," I told her.

"Uh-huh, I *know*. And Tally?"

"Yes?"

"This time try to wear it the *human* way."

You know how sometimes you have a song stuck in your head and you don't know how it got there? Sometimes it works the same way with memories. And right after Nadia left, for some reason I couldn't stop thinking about an incredibly fun day at the end of fifth grade, when Dad took Spider and me to an amusement park, and we got drenched on the water rides. Spider stayed over at our house that night; Dad set up a tent for us in the backyard, and we caught fireflies and roasted marshmallows.

A little while afterward, Mrs. Nevins started inventing reasons we couldn't hang out after school: *Oh, Caleb has a dentist appointment. Sorry, Caleb needs to clean his room.* Even if Spider argued about it, she wouldn't budge. A few months later, when she signed him up for stupid baseball, Mom invited her over to try to get her to change her mind. So of course I eavesdropped outside the kitchen, horrified as I heard Mrs. Nevins saying it was too late, she'd already picked up Caleb's uniform, and didn't Mom *really* think I should be hanging out with girls instead of Caleb? Not just for Caleb's sake, but for mine, she said.

When Mom answered that she was perfectly fine with me choosing my own friends, Mrs. Nevins sighed and said Mom didn't understand about boys, and that raising girls was so much easier.

Then she added: "Although shopping must be such a challenge. Especially with Tally."

Mom's voice grew sharp as she asked Mrs. Nevins exactly what she meant by that.

And Mrs. Nevins answered: "Oh, just that Tally's still a young girl, but she isn't very . . . *little*. And some of the cute styles the girls are wearing must look so *wrong* on her. You know, with her body type."

Mom replied with something I couldn't hear, and then dishes clattered in the sink. I could tell this meant Mom was kicking Mrs. Nevins out, so I ran upstairs to my room before they could notice me.

That was the first time I'd thought about my "body type." I mean, I always knew I was bigger and taller than the other kids in my grade, but I didn't think it meant anything about what clothes I could wear. Or *should* wear.

And the whole thing just infuriated me: Mrs. Nevins saying I should hang out with girls, but that I'd be "wrong" to dress like them. Well, who wanted to look like the other girls, anyway, I told myself. I wanted to look like *myself*, and I wanted that self to be friends with Caleb.

Although now, in seventh grade, we were in separate classes for most of the day, so being with him had gotten kind of complicated.

But the weekend Dad took us to the amusement park, nobody said it was weird that we were friends, or that we should hang out with different people. And probably I smiled more in those two days than I'd smiled in my entire life.

Shampoo

FIFTEEN MINUTES LATER, WE WERE all in the lobby wearing our lima bean–colored drooling-bulldog tees. Spider was one of the last kids to walk off the elevator, and for a few minutes I actually considered confronting Marco (*"All right, what have you done with him?"*).

But finally Spider appeared, looking calm and rested, as if he'd just had a refreshing nap.

As soon as he got off the elevator, I ran over to him. "Why didn't you answer your phone? I called and texted like fifteen times!"

"You did?" His eyes widened. "Oh, sorry. I was in the shower."

"*For an hour and a half?*"

"I shampooed," he said, as if that explained anything. "Hey, Tally, were you on the third floor looking for me?"

"Yeah. How'd you know?"

"Derrick Chen saw you. You shouldn't do that, okay? It's embarrassing."

Sonnet, who I hadn't even realized was standing behind me, poked my elbow as if to say: *See? I told you so.*

"Well, sorry, Spider," I said. "It was just because you weren't answering, and I thought maybe something was wrong with your phone."

"My phone? My phone is *fine*."

Something in his voice startled me. It was the first time I'd ever heard it, a hard edge.

And not knowing how to react to that sound, I just pretended I hadn't noticed.

"Okay, good," I told him. "That's a relief, then."

"All right, folks," Mr. G was saying. "We're going to stroll over to the National Mall as a group. *As a group.* You all know what 'as a group' means?"

"It means *no wandering off*," Mrs. Seeley announced.

She was in a completely new color-free outfit—pale gray top, pale gray scarf, white visor, big movie-star sunglasses—and carrying a large plastic cup of iced coffee.

I saw Mr. G and Ms. Jordan exchange a glance, which I suspected was about Mrs. Seeley's bossiness. Teachers out-ranked chaperones, but you could tell Mrs. Seeley didn't know that rule.

Mr. G smiled. "Yes, exactly. Thank you,. Mrs. Seeley. We have a three-quarters-of-a-mile walk to the mall, and the weather is great, so. let's keep a brisk pace, shall we? *¡Vámanos!*"

Roy stood at the revolving door as we filed out. "Enjoy our nation's capital," he said, waving his snake hand. I saluted, but he ignored me.

Ava, Nadia, Haley, Sydney Brunner, and Shanaya Hayes were the first ones out onto the muggy street, closely fol-lowed by Mrs. Seeley. Ms. Jordan and Mr. G stayed with the middle part of the group, along with Mia's and Althea's moms, while Sonnet, Spider, and I walked at the back, with Jamal's dad trailing us like Mr. Mallard in *Make Way for Ducklings*. But I wasn't worried about him eavesdropping on us because (a) why would he? and (b) he was wearing earbuds.

"So, how's it going with Marco?" I asked Spider, as if the question had just then occurred to me.

He shrugged. "Fine. He was in Trey's room the whole time."

"Well, that's good, right? That way he can't bother you."

"He isn't bothering me, actually."

"Awesome," I said enthusiastically. "And did you notice anything?"

"How could I? He wasn't there."

"But did you, you know, take advantage of the opportunity?" Since we were in public, I didn't want to specify what I meant, but it had to be obvious: the spy game. If Spider was actually playing.

"Tally, I told you, I was in the shower." Then Spider's face brightened. "But I did see what he left in the bathroom: baby shampoo."

"*Baby* shampoo? Oh, that's adorable!" Sonnet started giggling.

Adorable? I gave her a look.

"We're getting awesome data," I said, glancing behind to make sure Jamal's dad still couldn't hear us. "Haley brought a pink stuffed moose, and Ava doesn't eat sweets. *And* she keeps a notebook full of numbers."

"Numbers?" Spider repeated. He seemed interested. "Do you think it's some kind of code?"

"Possibly." I hadn't considered that. Ava was in accelerated math, but she never seemed like a numbers person to me. She wasn't even someone who seemed to *like* numbers, especially. "I mean, I didn't see any pattern, but—"

"Everything good, you guys?" All of a sudden, Ms. Jordan was beside the three of us. She was shiny again, not dusty and droopy like she'd looked when we arrived at the hotel, and her new-looking turquoise sneakers gave her a bouncy walk.

"Yep, everything's fine," I said.

"What's all that?" She pointed to my arms and legs. Since we were being forced to wear the Ugly Tee, I'd decided to decorate my limbs with pirate Band-Aids. I'd also stuck a couple on my neck.

"Mosquito bites," I said. "If I don't cover them up, I'll scratch, which can lead to infection."

"Oh yes. Washington's a swamp. I should have warned you guys there'd be mosquitoes."

"That's okay. I'm always prepared for mosquitoes and other random annoying creatures!"

Ms. Jordan gave me a funny look and jogged to the front.

Cheese

AS SOON AS WE ARRIVED at the National Mall, Sydney let out a wail. "Ms. Jordan, this can't be a mall. There aren't any shops!"

Ms. Jordan smiled. "In eighteenth-century England, the word 'mall' meant a 'shady promenade.' In other words, a tree-lined walkway."

"In other words, bor-ang," Sydney said.

"There's nothing boring about this place, dear," Mrs. Seeley told her. "It's the heart of the world's democracy."

Ms. Jordan kept on smiling at Mrs. Seeley. "Yes, although

let's remember that America didn't invent democracy. It's one of the many American things that had its origin somewhere else."

"Yeah, like hot dogs," Marco said. "Which are from Germany."

"And apple pie," Spider added.

I blinked. "Oh no, Spider, that's wrong! Apple pie is *definitely* American."

"Not originally," Spider insisted. He jutted his chin at me. "It's from England, like in the thirteen hundreds. I read it."

A hot wind blew up, snapping Ms. Jordan's hair around her face. "Yes, that's true, and plenty of other American foods are also on that list. Did you guys know the ancient Aztecs ate peanut butter and popcorn?"

"*¡Yupi!*" Nadia exclaimed. "My people rule!"

Haley laughed. "Nadia, you're not Aztec."

"No, but my family is Mexican-American, so I bet we're part Aztec, too. Do not doubt me, mortal." She stuck out her tongue, and I saw Haley, Ava, and Sonnet laugh.

My own hair started whipping around then, so I made a sort of bun out of it, holding it in place with one of my elastic fake-shark-tooth bracelets. Because I'm adopted, I didn't know my exact heritage, but I liked wondering about it. Sometimes I thought of myself as a mathematical formula:

> X (*Bio-mom Marisa, whose mom was from Portugal and whose dad was Italian-American*) + Y (*Bio-dad*) = *me, genetically speaking.*

Of course, Bio-mom Marisa wasn't just a simple sum of her own two parents; there were all these other unknown ancestors you had to add to the equation, who could have been from anywhere: Brazil. Morocco. Canada. And same for Bio-dad, whoever he was. So it really wasn't a straight addition equation, anyway. Or if it *was* an addition equation, it was the kind that was so big and complicated, it would take over an entire whiteboard.

Also, this formula didn't factor in Mom and Dad and Fiona—and, obviously, I was the product of them, too.

And sometimes I wondered: If you added up Marisa + Bio-dad + Mom + Dad, would the answer be Talia Martin—or would there still be something missing? Like my mathitude, for example: Did I get it from Bio-dad or Marisa? The little I knew about her didn't include any math scores. Mom and Dad both hated math, and Fiona almost failed ninth grade algebra last year. Maybe there was some specifically Tally math ability that just popped up all on its own—not a gene gift from anyone, just a 100-Percent Me thing.

Or maybe one day I'd meet Marisa and find out that all this time she was a nuclear physicist or a math teacher. Because it was possible, wasn't it? For all I knew, she even had a ringtail-lemur necklace like mine. And a big butt, too.

When I looked up, I saw Marco staring at my hair, as if bun-making were a complicated math problem he wanted to watch me solve.

We started at the Lincoln Memorial, which Mr. G said was the site of Martin Luther King's "I Have a Dream" speech on August 28, 1963.

I wanted to breathe the air around the Abraham Lincoln statue, feel historic molecules blowing on my skin. But immediately Mrs. Seeley announced that it was the "ideal spot for a group photo," so she organized us on the steps and took out a camera—a real camera, not a phone.

"Let's see those beautiful T-shirts," she insisted. "And let's have everybody smiling. Say 'cheese'!"

Nobody said it.

"Come on, what's the matter with saying 'cheese'?" she argued, laughing.

"Too cheesy," Marco said.

"How about if we say, 'Go, Bulldogs'?" Nadia suggested.

"Or just 'Eastview,'" Ava said. "You have to smile when you say 'East.'"

Everyone liked that, so they shouted "Eastview." But not me. I was disgusted: Saying "Eastview" at the Lincoln Memorial pretty much wrecked the aura of the whole place, as far as I was concerned. So instead I shouted, "I have a dream," which meant I finished a nanosecond after everyone. It came out "Eastview . . . a dream," and that made everybody giggle hysterically.

Except for Ms. Jordan, who held up a hand. "Can we get one more photo? And this time, can everyone follow Tally's example and say 'dream'?"

"Oh, that's wonderful," Mrs. Seeley exclaimed. "Okay, everybody. Ava, darling, get your hair out of your eyes. And stand up straight, please! One, two, three—"

"Dream!" everyone shouted.

"Cheese," I said. Because I hated the idea of turning Dr. King's speech into a photo opportunity. And everyone saying the word "dream" as if it meant "smile."

Selfies

NEXT WE WALKED OVER TO the Vietnam Memorial. As soon as I saw it, I had a weird feeling in my stomach, like how it felt when Grandma Wendy died and we went to the cemetery. A feeling like I wanted to cry, or something, but also like it was wrong to make any sounds.

I guessed other people felt like that too, because the whole place was pretty quiet. We watched a woman hold a sheet of paper to the wall, and use a pencil to make a rubbing of the name. *Who was that person,* I wondered. Her husband? No, she wasn't old enough. Her father? Uncle?

Whoever it was, she loved that person; you could tell by the way her fingers stayed on the name.

Finally, she slipped the paper into her bag and left. Then Mr. G told us that that there'd been a national contest to see who could design a memorial for the Vietnam War, and the winner was a college student named Maya Lin.

"Why do you think she designed it this way?" he asked.

"It's such a weird shape," Ava said, frowning. "It's not even a right angle."

It was such an Ava thing to say—but the thing was, she was right. I looked it up on my phone: the two sides met at an angle of 125 degrees 12 minutes, a funny angle to choose, really. Plus, those extra twelve-sixtieths of a degree definitely bothered me. Why did we need them? Monuments were supposed to be *exact*.

"Also," Nadia said, "the names aren't even alphabetical."

"Right," Ms. Jordan said. "Maya Lin decided to list the names chronologically, in order of when each soldier fell or went missing in action. Why do you think she made that choice?"

"To make you search for them?" Spider called out.

I stared. Spider wasn't in my social studies class this year, so I never saw him answer questions. Last year, he barely said a word unless the teacher made him. And even then, he'd say like three syllables.

Mr. G was smiling at Spider. "And why do you think she wanted that?"

"I don't know," Spider said. "Maybe so you can't just *come* here; you have to *do* something."

"Interesting," Mr. G said.

"But even if you come here looking for just one name, the chronological order causes you to see *other* names too. How they're all connected," Ms. Jordan added.

She caught my eye for a second. What was that about?

I looked away, pretending to focus on un-bunning my hair.

"Didn't a lot of people protest the war?" Spider asked. "So maybe Maya Lin wanted people to spend time here. To bring them together, kind of."

Mr. G gave Spider a high five. "Monuments can remind us that we're one nation. *E pluribus unum,* right? And very smart thinking there, Caleb."

Spider beamed.

So did I. It was great how Mr. G had praised Spider in front of everybody. And it was also great how Spider spoke up, especially about something he didn't know for sure.

Because Spider collected facts about his favorite subjects, but when you asked for his opinion, he usually just shrugged. So seeing him be brave enough to guess—especially in public—made me very happy.

But then two things happened to spoil my good mood:

The first was that Mr. G raised his eyebrows at me and smiled. This gave me a weird feeling, because it was like he was saying: *Did you hear your friend just now?* And of course I had. Why would he think I hadn't?

The second was that all of a sudden, Ava, Nadia, Haley, Sydney, Shanaya, and some other girls started posing for selfies. Like they thought the whole function of the wall was to serve as a backdrop for their outfits and hairstyles. And then Mrs. Seeley took out her camera and actually encouraged them to pose: *"Look at me, everyone, and squeeze together. Ava honey, hands by your side, and no squinting, please."*

And maybe the worst part was that Sonnet wanted to join them. Haley Spriggs was waving her over, and she asked if I thought she should go.

"You mean to photobomb it?" I said.

"No, I mean to be *in* the photo. *With* them." Her cheeks were pink.

"Sonnet, if you want to, just do it."

"You won't mind?"

"Are you crazy? Why would I *mind*?"

Immediately she ran over to squeeze herself next to Haley.

Out of nowhere, Ms. Jordan appeared by my side. "Tally, don't you want to be in the photo?"

"You mean, why don't I want to be in some stupid photo that basically misses the point of this entire monument? Just like we missed the point of the Lincoln Memorial?"

"Okay, I get what you're saying, and I don't disagree. These are solemn, important places in our history. But don't you think a photo would be a nice souvenir from the trip? And one day you'll look back—"

"And I'll think: Who are those girls, and why are they *smiling* in front of the Vietnam Memorial? Don't they understand what it's about? And why do they all look exactly the same?"

"Why? Because they're all wearing Eastview Spirit tees."

"Well, *yeah*. What I mean is, why are they all making exactly the same face?" I did The Smile for her. I even flipped my hair over my shoulder, the way Nadia did. Except my own hair didn't pose; it just blew into my face.

Ms. Jordan patted my back. "All right, Tally, I get your

point. You're a strong individual, and that's great sometimes. But being part of a group is *also* great sometimes. There would be no Civil Rights Movement if people hadn't joined forces, right? Same thing for the anti–Vietnam War movement. And the American Revolution, too, for that matter. Think about what I was saying before, how the names on this wall are all connected."

Okay, this was getting way too history-lessonish for me. All I'd meant was that I didn't want to be in the clonegirl photo. Why did Ms. Jordan care about it, anyway?

And now she was squinting at my sweaty arms.

"You're losing Band-Aids," she explained, pointing to the pirate Band-Aid flapping off my elbow, exposing mosquito-biteless skin.

I pressed the Band-Aid back on. "Oops. Thanks."

"You're welcome."

For a second I thought she'd ask why I was wearing Band-Aids if my skin was obviously unbitten. But I was relieved she didn't, because the truth was I didn't even know.

My Idea of Perfect

WE DID MORE MEMORIALS—World War II, Korean War, FDR—and then people started complaining about being hungry and tired.

"Okay, time for dinner," Ms. Jordan agreed. "But first, a moment for the Washington Monument, which we can't visit at the moment due to some renovation. But let's all gaze at it from afar. Who knows what we call its shape? Tally?" She smiled at me, knowing I knew the answer.

"An obelisk," I announced. "Which means it has a square or rectangle bottom and a pyramid top. So it's like a cross between two different polygons, which is really cool. And you know what else is cool? It's exactly five hundred fifty-five feet, five inches tall."

"No, it's not," Shanaya said.

"*Excuse* me?" I squinted at her.

"Since the earthquake, it's five hundred fifty-four feet, seven and eleven-thirty-seconds inches." She held up some article on her phone.

"Yeah," Spider chimed in. "And *before* the earthquake, it was five hundred fifty-five feet, five and one-eighth inches. So actually, it was *always* off a little." He shrugged.

"Dude," Marco said. "Did you just, like, *know* that?"

Because the thing was, unlike Shanaya, Spider wasn't even reading this number off his phone.

My cheeks burned. It had really bothered me that the Vietnam Memorial had that weird angle, and I definitely did *not* want to hear all those messy fractions about the Washington Monument, which had always been my idea of perfect. And why was Spider agreeing with Shanaya? I knew he wouldn't make me look dumb in front of everyone on purpose, but I wondered why he didn't just tell me this fact in private. I mean, if he had it in his head the whole time, anyway.

Ms. Jordan caught my eye. "Well, as Tally informs me, the Washington Monument is the world's tallest freestanding obelisk *and* the world's tallest stone structure, so how cool is *that*?" She gave me a thumbs-up. So I felt maybe one lepton better. A lepton and a half.

Then we trooped back to Hotel Independence, where we could eat half-price in the Thomas Jefferson restaurant. (Or, at least, that was the deal they'd offered the imaginary medical-school students, and they were probably too scared of Mrs. Seeley not to offer it to us.)

"Oh, yummy, Revolutionary War food," I said. "Porridge and lard, probably, right?"

"And venison," Spider said.

"*Venison?*" My mouth dropped open. "Eww, I absolutely refuse to eat Bambi! Or Thumper! Or squirrel meat!"

"Shh, Tally," Ms. Jordan scolded, even though we were just walking on a noisy city street. "I'm sure the restaurant has regular, delicious, modern food. And it's buffet style, so just choose whatever you want."

"You mean it's all-you-can-eat?" asked Trey, his eyes popping. "I'm so hungry I'm gonna eat till it's coming out of my eyeballs."

Nadia slapped Trey's arm. "Try not to be disgusting, okay?"

"Sorry. But it's not *my* fault boys need to eat. Maybe *girls* don't, but—"

"Who *says* girls don't?" I challenged him. Marco smiled; I pretended not to see.

"Let's *all* not take more than we'll eat," Ms. Jordan said. "Let's act like well-mannered hotel guests, shall we?"

Ava mumbled something to Nadia that I couldn't hear.

Body Talk

A FEW MINUTES LATER WE entered the restaurant. It was less American Revolution-y than the rest of the hotel, but still red, white, and blue, with fancy portraits on the walls, and tiny colonial flags on all the tables instead of flower vases or candles. But I was relieved to see that the buffet thing worked kind of like the school cafeteria—except without sporks or lunch ladies in hairnets or lukewarm sour-smelling milk in half-pint containers.

Also, the food looked good. I mean, really good. On my plate I heaped some stir-fried chicken dish, a mini-pizza, peas with almonds, and some apple pie. Sonnet had mac and cheese and french fries; Spider had mashed potatoes and a chili dog. The three of us grabbed a big table by the dessert stand and started stuffing our mouths. I hadn't realized how hungry I was, but as soon as I started eating, I realized that I hadn't had a real meal all day.

"Hey, Tally, remember that time your family took us to that street fair and we had like three hot dogs each?" Spider said. "And then all of a sudden I asked: Why are they called hot dogs?"

"So Dad had to explain they were just the shape of dachshunds, and weren't actual *dog*," I said. "And finally you believed him."

"Yeah. I was so dumb."

I patted his arm "You weren't dumb; you were little."

"I used to think horseradish was made from horses," Sonnet said. "And once my mom made chicken cacciatore, and I freaked because I thought it was made out of cats."

"That's terrible," Spider said, laughing.

"You know those pastries called bear claws and elephant ears?" I said. "Guess what I thought when Dad first baked some."

"Eww," Spider said, laughing.

"Good thing he never made ladyfingers." I grinned at Spider, who was laughing even harder now, a *hyuk-hyuk* that made his shoulders go sideways. Suddenly I realized that I hadn't heard that laugh in a long time.

Then a strange thing happened. Haley, Nadia, and Ava asked if they could join us. Or, rather, Haley asked Sonnet, and Nadia and Ava were somehow included in the question.

"Sure," Sonnet said ecstatically, scooching over toward me to make room for the three of them. Which meant she was now bumping her elbow into mine every time she picked up her fork.

"So how's the food?" Nadia asked.

"Pretty good," Sonnet said.

"Shockingly delectable," I answered with a full mouth. "I may go back for some of that mac and cheese."

"Really?" Nadia said. "Omigod, Tally. How much can you eat?"

"A possibly infinite amount, especially after all those memorials. Although I have to say this apple pie isn't one-fifth as good as my dad's."

While I was saying this, Spider caught my eye, touching his lower lip a few times, which I took to mean, *Tally, wipe your face.* So I did, immediately realizing I had a speck of apple-pie crust on my chin.

And then I noticed Ava's plate. She'd taken a parallelogram of lasagna, a Red Delicious apple, and some salad without dressing. The funny thing was the lasagna, because noodles were carbs, weren't they? Supposedly Ava didn't do carbs. I considered pointing out to her the inconsistency of eating lasagna a few hours after refusing my dad's carb-full Baked Goodies. But Ava took one small bite, chewed slowly, and pushed her plate away.

"I don't even know why I took all that stuff," she said. "I'm really not the teeniest bit hungry."

"You always say that, Ava," Nadia said.

"Well, it's true."

"It can't *always* be true. Not *literally.*"

Ava's face pinched. "Nadia, stop bugging me, all right? I'll eat what I want."

"In other words, nothing."

"Want a french fry?" Sonnet offered. "You don't have to be hungry to eat fries."

Ava smiled. "No thanks, Sonnet. I never eat fried food."

"Why not?" I asked.

"I have a sensitive stomach."

I took a fry from Sonnet's plate. "Oh well, more for the rest of us, right?"

"Not me," Nadia said. "I have no self-control. If I eat one fry, I'll eat the whole plate. Literally! Also the silverware. And the tablecloth."

"Come on, Nadia, you're not even close to fat," Haley said as she nibbled her hamburger.

"But I could *get* fat. Fat is genetic, and omigod, you guys should see my mom's butt."

Haley giggled. "I *have* seen it, and it's a totally normal mom-sized butt. And seriously, if anyone should worry about getting fat, it's me."

"You?" Sonnet said in disbelief. "You're so skinny, Haley."

"That's what *you* think. My thigh gap disappeared over the summer."

"What's a thigh gap?" I asked.

"What it sounds like," Nadia snapped.

Haley didn't even look at me. "Seriously, you guys, I'm just *squish*. My arms are balloons, my hips bulge out, and my belly is, like, disgusting. This summer I had to throw out all my favorite skinny pants."

"Come on, I'm sure you're exaggerating," Sonnet said.

"You think so? I'll show you in the room later, Sonnet. You'll be *horrified*."

"When I do jumping jacks, everything jiggles," I announced. "It's pretty funny, actually."

"I'm sure it is, Tally," Nadia said. She took a bite of hamburger.

"Anyhow, what's the big deal about butt size?" I continued. "I have a *gigantic* butt. Who cares?"

No one said anything. Sonnet was pink, for some weird reason.

"Okay, well, I'm off," Spider muttered, looking only at me.

"Wait, you're leaving? Where are you going?" I asked.

"Up to the room to watch TV," he answered. "Or maybe read. Anyway. Bye." He hurried off with his plate.

"Poor Spider," Haley said. "All that body talk must have freaked him out."

"Well, if he hangs out with girls all the time, what does he expect?" Nadia said.

I was appalled. "Excuse me, Sonnet and I talk about *plenty* of things besides how fat we are. Which, if you ask me, is a bleeping *boring* topic."

Ava raised her eyebrows. "Oh, really, Tally? And what fascinating topics do *you* discuss?"

"Regular things," Sonnet answered quickly. "You know. People, school, movies, music—"

"I'm sure you discuss fashion, right?" Nadia said, laughing as she eyed my remaining Band-Aids. By then, most had slid off with my sweat, but I still had one on my neck and another on my wrist.

Haley started giggling again, but she tried to hide it behind her napkin.

"I can assure you," I said loudly, "that we *never* discuss fashion."

"I can assure you that I'm not surprised," Nadia replied.

"In fact, we discuss *far* more interesting topics than the ones Sonnet mentioned. Like math, for example."

"You talk about *math*?" Ava asked.

"Not really," Sonnet said.

"Constantly," I insisted. "For example, just the other day we were discussing the difference between a googol and a googolplex. Do you know what it is? You don't? All right, I'll tell you: A googol is a one with a hundred zeroes after it, and a googolplex is a one with a *googol* zeroes after it."

Dead silence.

"Also pi, as opposed to apple pie," I said. "Which I can currently recite to forty-six digits. My short-term goal is fifty-five, but I'm aiming for one hundred."

"Tally," Nadia said, plucking a french fry off Sonnet's plate, "you're the all-time weirdest person in human history."

"I'll take that as a compliment," I replied, bowing my head. "Deepest thanks."

"Well, doesn't that all look scrumptious." Mrs. Seeley was standing by our table holding a plate heaped with salad. "May I squeeze in with you girls?"

"Sure, there's plenty of room," Sonnet said, as if somehow she'd become the host. "Besides, Mrs. Seeley, you're so skinny."

I gave Sonnet a look like: *You did* not *just say that.*

Mrs. Seeley beamed as she took over Spider's chair. "That's so sweet of you, dear. But I didn't used to be. Has Ava told you?"

"Told us what?" Sonnet asked eagerly. I poked my elbow into her side, but she didn't react.

Ava put down her fork. "Mom used to be a little overweight," she said.

Mrs. Seeley chuckled. "You're understating it, sweetheart. I was *obese*. But one day about five years ago, I decided to lose the weight and get healthy. Because the business world can be very harsh on women." She pierced a cherry tomato with her fork.

"That's so cool," Nadia said. "I wish my mom could be like you."

"Oh, she can be, honey. Tell her to call me anytime and I'll do a free wardrobe critique, the works. Ava, you didn't like your dinner?"

Ava shrugged. "I'm not hungry."

"Well, you need to eat *something* after all that walking."

"Mom, I'll eat later, okay?"

"How? It's not like you have access to a full refrigerator here."

"If I'm hungry later, that's *my* problem," Ava muttered.

I looked up. Was I the only person who thought things at this table had turned a bit awkward, even more awkward than before? I couldn't tell; no one would meet my eyes, not even Sonnet.

"Hey, I have an idea," Sonnet was saying brightly. "What if you asked for a doggy bag, Ava? Then you could bring the food up to your room and just eat when you want."

"I guess," Ava said, not enthusiastically.

"Sonnet, that's an excellent idea," Mrs. Seeley exclaimed. She sprung up from the table and returned a minute later with a plastic takeout container, the kind with a lid. Then she lifted the lasagna and the salad off Ava's plate and arranged them carefully in the plastic container. If she'd had tiny hangers, she'd have used them, I bet.

"There," she said. "Perfect. Thanks for thinking of this, Sonnet."

"You're welcome," Sonnet said, smiling.

Ava stood. "Okay, so I'll take all this back to the room now, I guess. See you guys later."

"Wait, honey," Mrs. Seeley said. "You're going to drill your French adverbs tonight, right?"

"Of *course*, Mom. Do I ever forget?"

She air-kissed her mom's cheek and fled the Thomas Jefferson.

The Manicure

THAT NIGHT I ENDED UP watching a movie with Nadia and Haley. I know how crazy that sounds, believe me—but it happened only because Haley invited Sonnet, and I could see that Sonnet desperately wanted to accept. But I knew she'd hang with me instead, out of loyalty, and I didn't like thinking I was some kind of charity.

So I pretended not to realize that Haley had snubbed me. "That sounds like a great idea!" I said. "What movie should we see?"

Nadia and Haley gave each other a look, but they didn't ban me from participation.

We snatched some cookies from the dessert stand and snuck them upstairs to Haley and Sonnet's room. Nadia grabbed the remote and started channel-surfing. Finally the three of them agreed on some ultra-insipid rom com called *The Manicure*, about a woman who falls in love with her male nail polisher for some reason I couldn't follow.

After about twenty minutes of watching this woman decide if she was going to ask Nail Polish Guy to some kind of fancy snobby business party, I gave up.

"You know what this movie desperately needs?" I said. "A giant tub of greasy popcorn."

"Shh, Tally," Haley said.

"Well, sorry. But you can't do movies without popcorn. It's practically un-American."

"Un-Aztec," Nadia reminded me.

"Well, *whoever* invented popcorn, I can't watch a movie without it," I declared.

"Then don't," Nadia said, staring at the TV.

So I texted Spider: Hey how's it going? I'm being subjected to movie torture. At first he didn't answer, and I despaired that he was shampooing again.

But about fifteen minutes later he texted: I'm fine & guess what, Marco uses bubble gum flavored mouthwash

Me: EWW. For what?

Spider: IDK, to fight tooth decay? Or to kill ants?

Me: Bleh, poor ants. But it goes with the baby shampoo. Does Marco also wear diapers??

I waited, but Spider didn't text back. Which was odd. At ten, there was a knock on the door. Haley jumped off the bed to answer.

It was Ms. Jordan, who poked her head into the room. "Good movie, girls?"

"Oh, it's great!" Haley said. "We're watching *The Manicure*. Have you seen it?"

"No, I guess I missed that one." She grinned in a way that made me think she shared my opinion, at least of this one stupid movie. "Where's Ava?"

We all looked at each other. Ava had said she'd see us later, but I wondered if she even knew we were watching a movie. She'd left the restaurant before we'd made our plan for the evening. For all I knew, this whole time she'd been back in our room, studying French adverbs.

"I'm guessing she went to bed early," Haley said. "She seemed a little tired at dinner."

"And grumpy," Nadia added. "Although she's *always* grumpy lately."

"Okay, well, sorry to break this up, girls, but I'm afraid it's lights-out time," Ms. Jordan said.

"Seriously?" Nadia scrunched her face in disbelief.

"You don't have to go to bed now, just go back to your rooms. But I'd strongly suggest getting some sleep—we need to be awake and downstairs having breakfast by seven. Full day of action!"

"What are we doing tomorrow?" Haley asked.

Ms. Jordan smiled. "The afternoon is the Capitol tour. We're trying to arrange something special for the morning, but I don't want to say until we know it's for sure. Good night!" She waved and moved on to the next room.

I rolled off the bed. "Ooh, I love mysteries. Better than rom coms, truthfully."

"Well, no one was forcing you to watch it with us, Tally," Nadia said.

I glanced at Sonnet, who was studying her cuticles.

Counting

I PUT THE KEY CARD in my door, expecting to see Ava propped up on her pillows with French-adverb flash cards. But the room was dark, and when I turned on the bathroom light, I could see that Ava's bed was empty. Also completely undisturbed. There was no sign that she'd even come back to the room after leaving the restaurant—except for one thing: The plastic container of uneaten food was in the trash.

Where was she? Possibly in her mom's room, I thought—although after the way Ava had behaved at the table, it was hard to imagine her wanting to hang out with Mrs. Seeley all night. Maybe she'd gone to her mom's room to apologize. Well, wherever she was, it was good to have the room to myself.

The first thing I did was kick off my shoes, which happened to be cowboy boots. I did a few jumping jacks, watching myself jiggle in the mirror. Did I need a new bra? I guess I did; I'd mention it to Mom when I got home. She'd probably just buy me whatever kind was on sale at Kohl's. I bet Mrs. Seeley bought Ava underwear at some fancy boutique in the city, the same sort of place where she bought all Ava's clothes.

And suddenly I felt a sort of prickle of curiosity about Ava's clothes. If I was really still playing this spy game, I needed more data, didn't I?

I opened the top drawer of Ava's dresser: A bunch of tees all lined up, shoulders touching. Two pairs of black biker shorts, folded exactly in half. And socks, rolled-up like unbaked croissants on a bakery shelf. What must it be like to be Ava, so careful and perfect, even about things that were supposed to be private? To be honest, I couldn't imagine.

Before I closed the drawer, I made sure nothing looked poked or rearranged; knowing Ava, she'd accuse me if even one sock was out of place. I wondered if Ava was naturally so crazy organized, or if she'd learned it from her mom. Maybe Mrs. Seeley did drawer inspections, and punished Ava if her underwear wasn't alphabetized. It wouldn't surprise me, truthfully. How could she live with a mom like that? *I* certainly couldn't, that was for sure. For the first time ever, I thought it would be hard to be Ava Seeley.

The drawer beneath was a teeny bit open, so I tugged on the knob. More of Ava's stuff, mostly tops and sweaters. With the edges of my fingertips, I held up a pale blue-gray sweater Ava sometimes wore. It was softer than any of mine, maybe the softest thing I'd ever felt, if you didn't count Spike's ears. I checked the label: 100 percent cashmere. Whoa. Not a kid material. And definitely not something they sold at Kohl's. No way would Mom buy me something like this. Or buy it for herself, come to think of it. The Seeleys had money to spend on fancy clothes. Well, woo-hoo for them.

I held the sweater over my chest and looked in the mirror. On me it looked like a bib. I put it back.

Underneath the sweater was a tank top the color of calamine lotion. Which looked pretty standard for clonegirl-wear, except it was made of some kind of superhero-costume material that stretched like Silly Putty. I mean, this tank fit Ava, obviously, but the way it stretched, I could tell it would probably fit me, too.

I slipped it over my head and looked in the mirror. The

tank squished my boobs, and didn't even make it down to my belly button, but I was *in* it. That was *me* in the mirror. Wearing calamine-lotion pink, a color I never wore, ever.

Talia Martin fits into Ava Seeley's clothes, hahaha! Take that, all you snotty clonegirls!

Still wearing the tank, I went into the bathroom. Ava had lined up her bottles on the edge of the sink: shampoo, after-shampoo lotion, pre-blow-drying conditioner, after-blow-drying conditioner. Egads, what a ritual—if I had to remember all those steps, I'd just shave my head and be done with it.

Next to the bottles was a vinyl bag covered with yellow daisies. It had a million zippers, and all of them were closed; on the other hand, she'd left the bag out here in public. Well, this was a bathroom, so not *in public*—but if she'd wanted to keep the bag ultra-private, she could have stuck it in a drawer or something, right? I mean, she knew I'd be using the bathroom. And there wasn't a sign on the bag that said NO PEEKING.

So I unzipped it. Every zipper.

But it was mostly stuff you'd expect: a retainer, some lip gloss, ponytail holders, a nail file, bobby pins, zit wipes. The fact that she used zit wipes was a little bit spy-worthy; but maybe she had them in the unlikely event she had a break-out, which she never did. Although she also had a small tube of concealer—and why would you need concealer if you had nothing to conceal?

Thinking of secret zits and then secrets in general, I remembered Ava's tiny yellow notebook with all the numbers. Had she added any more? I left the bathroom and searched her bed, and under her pillow, the last place I'd seen it. But it wasn't there. Maybe she'd stuck it on the nightstand, under her dumb fashion magazines. Or inside the drawer . . . ?

Ta-da. There it was.

I opened the notebook to the same page as before:

65

200?

12

approx 150

25

10

Was Spider's guess right—was it some kind of code? As a math person, I was usually good at picking up number patterns—but if there was a pattern here, I didn't see it. All the numbers were divisible by five, except for the 12. And two of the numbers were divisible by ten, which made them seem rounded off; in fact, the 200 had a question mark, and the 150 had the abbreviation "approx." So it was odd that the 12 was so specific. A dozen *what*?

Another strange thing: Some days had more numbers than others, some pages were almost blank, every page had a date, and Ava hadn't missed a day since last May.

And that 10 was new—the first time I'd peeked, there'd been only five numbers, but now there were six. Did all the pages have six? I flipped through the notebook: Some pages had four numbers; some had seven or eight; a couple had two. One had none, but it had a gold star at the top. She'd given herself a gold star for what? Getting all her French adverbs right? Alphabetizing socks?

A faint rustling sound was coming from the hallway outside the door. Was that Ava? *Bleep.*

I yanked off the tank, stuffed it under my pillow, tossed Ava's notebook back in the drawer, and started jumping.

Ava dragged herself into the room, looking sweaty and red-faced. She was wearing a big, loose tee and gray sweat-pants that said PENN STATE UNIVERSITY down one leg. "Hey," she said. "What are you doing?"

"Jumping jacks," I said breathlessly. "Where were you?"

"In the hotel gym."

"This whole time?"

"Yeah. Why? Is that a problem?"

"For me? No." I stopped jumping; my boobs were hurting. Yeah, I definitely did need a new bra. I put my top back on and sat on the bed, my heart thumping. "We were wondering what happened to you."

"'We'?"

"Haley, Nadia, Sonnet. And I."

She blinked. "You were all *together*?"

"Uh-huh. Why? Is that so shocking?"

"Yeah, actually. It is." Ava sat on the floor, her chin on her knees. Then she lay down and took a deep breath. "Haley and Nadia aren't your friends, you know."

I decided to ignore that. "Well, we were watching a movie in Sonnet's room. And Haley's. It was really dumb."

"Sorry I missed it, then. I love bad movies." She started doing sit-ups.

"Why are you doing sit-ups?" I asked.

"Because I always do before bed."

"But aren't you tired after the gym?"

"Shut up, Tally, okay? I'm counting."

I watched her for a while. Perfect sit-up form, of course. Perfect rhythm. If you were graded for sit-ups, she'd get a gold star.

Then something occurred to me. "Do you always count?"

"The sit-ups? Yeah."

"How many do you do?"

"Usually one hundred, but it varies. Why?"

"Just wondering. And you did other exercises in the gym just now?"

"Yeah, well, that's usually what you do in a gym, isn't it?"

"And you counted those, too?"

"Tally, why do you always have so many questions?"

"Sorry. I just never knew anyone so . . . organized."

"I assume you mean that as an insult."

"No. Not at all. Why is that an insult?"

"Because you'd never say it to me otherwise." She finished, finally, so she stood, panting. "I'm taking a shower now. Are you done in the bathroom?"

I hadn't even brushed my teeth, but I was stung by her comment. *I'd* insulted *Ava*? *She'd* insulted *me*. "Sure, go ahead," I said.

I said it nicely, in a friendly voice, but she still slammed the bathroom door behind her.

The Numbers

I WENT TO SLEEP DISAPPOINTED. Because the mystery of the tiny yellow notebook had been solved: Obviously, Ava had been recording her exercises, how many reps she'd done. Although I wondered why some numbers were only "approx" or followed by question marks. It was hard to believe, knowing her, that she'd lost count of her sit-ups. And what did it mean that she'd given herself a gold star on a blank page? Good job for *not* exercising? What sense did *that* make?

Even with all these questions, I was convinced I now

knew the meaning of the numbers. It wasn't fascinating, but at least I had spy stuff to report to Spider and Sonnet. I set the alarm on my phone for six a.m. so I could take a shower, and I fell asleep before Ava finished in the bathroom.

The next morning, when my phone buzzed, Ava was already awake, doing more sit-ups. She had earbuds on, and I guessed she hadn't heard my alarm. And probably the exercise zoned her out, because when I said good morning, she kind of flinched. So I apologized.

"It's fine," she muttered. "I just always do these in private."

"Every single morning?" I yawned loudly.

"Uh-huh."

"Wow. All those exercises at night and then you wake up and do more?"

"Yep."

"How come?"

"Because they're good for my body. Ever since I quit gymnastics, I've become a fat slug."

I had to laugh. "I'm sorry, *you*?"

"And they make me feel better, okay? Seriously, Tally. Are you going to start questioning me all the time now, like Nadia?"

"No. I mean, I didn't know Nadia was questioning you."

"Well, she is, and it's incredibly annoying. Although, truthfully, I think she's just jealous."

"Of what?"

"My weight. Because she's pre-fat. Don't tell anyone I said so."

"Of course not. Why would I?"

"Just making sure. Now will you *please* stop talking, so I can concentrate?"

"Sure," I said. "Concentrate all you like."

Then, for the first time since we'd walked into the hotel room—for the first time ever, really—I took a close-up look at Ava's body. She'd changed out of her pj's or whatever she'd slept in, into a snug cami and biker shorts. And it took my brain an extra second to process what I was seeing.

Whenever girls talk about how skinny or fat they are, I always zone out, because it's the kind of clonegirl talk that makes me want to throw heavy objects off rooftops. *Because, seriously, who the bleep cares?* I never secretly weigh other people; it would never occur to me to go, *Oh, she's way too fat to wear those jeans or that sweater* or whatever.

As for me, I never obsessed about my body, which was just this thing I got from Bio-mom. (Bio-dad too, obviously, whatever he looked like.)

And I knew that some people were just born skinny, and stayed that way, no matter what they ate—like Fiona, for example. But Ava's kind of skinny was a whole different category. With her just a few feet away from me on the hotel carpeting, straining to touch her elbows to her knees, I could see that she wasn't "slim" or "thin" or "petite," any of the normal words people used to describe bodies. The word for her was "emaciated," like Spike before I rescued her from the animal shelter.

Under her cami, Ava's ribs stuck out. When she did a sit-up, you could see every bone in her spine. Her arms looked like twigs, and her legs had a hollowed-out, diamond-shaped space between them—the "thigh gap" Haley was talking about, I guessed. Except this wasn't just a gap. It was a space as big as a cantaloupe.

What I'm saying is that Ava was scary skinny. Was I the only person who saw it? Did any of her friends realize how she looked underneath clothes? If Nadia did, she couldn't possibly be "jealous." And did Mrs. Seeley see? Who was her *mom*, so if she saw (and I couldn't imagine how she couldn't), why didn't she do something? Take Ava to a doctor, at the very least.

Although maybe she had. Maybe Ava had some Terrible

Disease that was making her look like this, and it was incurable, and there was nothing Mrs. Seeley could do but watch her daughter waste away.

But if Ava did have a Terrible Disease, how could she be doing all these sit-ups? Plus all that other stuff at the gym. Every day. Morning and night.

Was something wrong with Ava Seeley?

But there couldn't be. She had too much energy. And too much meanness.

"One hundred," Ava announced. She stayed on the carpeting for a minute, panting. Then she got up slowly, her face sweaty and pale. "Dibs on the shower."

"Go for it," I said. I rubbed my eyes to suggest they hadn't been focused, that I hadn't noticed how she looked just now. Hadn't been spying on her at all.

Angel

AVA CLOSED THE BATHROOM DOOR behind her. When I heard her turn on the shower, I grabbed the tank top from underneath my pillow, smoothed it out, folded it, opened Ava's drawer, and slipped it underneath the cashmere sweater.

Then I sat on the edge of my bed and tried to think. Maybe I should say something to her. Like what? Knowing Ava, she'd never listen to me, anyway. And telling my friends what I'd seen just felt wrong: This wasn't just more data for the spy game, which suddenly felt stupid and immature.

I told myself: *It's crazy to worry about someone who hates you!* And why was I always taking care of other people? Sometimes they didn't even appreciate it. Sometimes it even made them embarrassed, or annoyed. Seriously, I should be focusing on *me* for a change!

I got out my treasure box. Just looking at Grandma Wendy's old stuff cheered me up a little, as I considered what to wear for the day's Mystery Activity. Finally I decided on the mustache earrings and Grandma Wendy's green cat's-eye glasses with the rhinestones. The glasses felt a little slippery on my nose, which is why I never wore them. But seriously, they were supercool, I thought, as I checked myself out in the big mirror. Although they needed something else to complete the look. The purple newsboy cap? Maybe a scarf?

"Tally, what's that on your face?" Ava was standing in the room wrapped in a white hotel towel, dripping.

"You like?" I batted my eyes at her.

She laughed uncertainly. "Are you joking?"

"Exactly," I said. "I dress to amuse myself."

"Yeah, well. Glad you think you're so funny. But don't you care that everyone else is laughing at you?"

"*I'm* laughing at me. So *they* are irrelevant."

"If you say so."

She opened her drawers and pulled out a beige sweater.

For a second I panicked: Could she tell I'd been in there, snooping? But she didn't seem suspicious at all. She shut herself back in the bathroom to get dressed.

A few minutes later she came out wearing a short flowery skirt that showed her twiggy legs, and the beige sweater that let you almost see how skinny she was. Almost.

"Nice outfit," I said.

"Thanks," she replied airily. "Your turn in the bathroom."

I took a quick shower. The funny thing was, when I came back out into the bedroom, Ava was still in the room.

"Sorry I said that before," she muttered, as if someone were forcing her to apologize.

"Said what?" I asked innocently.

"You know. That people were laughing at you."

"No worries," I replied. "You dress like you, and I dress like me."

She watched me towel-dry my hair. I hadn't shampooed in the shower, but I had so much hair that it got itself wet.

"You want to borrow my blow-dryer? For your hair?" she asked.

"Nah. Never use one. But thanks," I added, wondering why she was offering. Maybe she felt guilty about what she'd said, but the thing was, she'd said stuff to me before that was way nastier. And it wasn't like I didn't *know* people were laughing at me. Really, I was kind of *daring* them to laugh.

She watched as I buttoned a big purple bowling shirt I'd discovered at someone's tag sale last summer. It had the word *Angel* on the pocket in a fancy script, which I knew was just some guy's name in Spanish—but I liked to imagine this was really an angel's shirt. If an angel went bowling.

"Okay, but you're not *really* going to wear that today, are you?" Ava said.

I blinked away some water droplets on my eyelashes. "Why not?"

"Because we've got the Capitol tour, and something else, possibly. Didn't you read the schedule?"

"Nope." I put on the mustache earrings.

"Well, at the bottom on page two there's an asterisk. And it says 'Please plan to dress appropriately.'"

"Appropriately for what? A solar eclipse? A zombie attack?"

Ava groaned. "Forget it, Tally. You're not going to listen to me, whatever I say. Isn't that right?"

"No, not necessarily," I said. "I mean, if you wanted to tell me something really important . . ."

"Like what?"

"I don't know. Maybe something personal." I met her eyes.

She looked away. "Why would I?"

"I don't know," I repeated. "But I'd listen. That's all I'm saying."

Three sharp raps on the door. "Girls, you all set for breakfast?"

It was Mrs. Seeley's voice, so Ava opened the door. At six thirty in the morning, Ava's mom looked wide awake and ready for business—navy blazer, white top, flowered scarf, gray skirt, gold jewelry, makeup.

"Good morning!" she shouted. "Ava, you look lovely. But I'm not too sure about that sweater."

Ava looked at her sweater. "What's wrong with it?"

"For one thing, it's wool, so you'll be too warm."

"No, I won't. And this hotel is freezing."

"You're cold? Really?" Mrs. Seeley frowned as if she doubted Ava's internal thermostat. "Well, the beige just washes you out."

"In my opinion, that sweater looks very nice on her," I announced.

Ava stared at me.

"*Your* opinion?" Mrs. Seeley smiled, flashing white

straight teeth. "Tally, dear, are those real glasses, or a costume?"

"They're actual frames. Just not actual lenses."

"Then why are you wearing them?"

"Because they're hilarious. Don't *you* think they are?"

"No, dear, to be honest. And I don't think they're appropriate for today's activities."

"Anyhow," Ava cut in loudly, "it's the only sweater I brought."

"Not true!" Mrs. Seeley protested. "You have plenty of others, plus that beautiful gray hoodie I hung in the closet—" Her phone rang. She checked the name and got excited. "Girls, I need to take this. I'll meet you downstairs at breakfast. Go on ahead."

She walked down the hall for better reception. "Yes, hi! So wonderful to hear from you!"

Then a strange thing happened.

Ava began walking toward the elevator. When I didn't follow, she turned around. "So are you coming, Tally?"

I hesitated. *Why was she asking me? Because I'd stood up to her mom about the sweater?*

"Don't you want to text your friends? So you can have breakfast together?" I asked. Instead of with *me*, I meant.

"That's okay. I'll see them downstairs," Ava said. "I'm starving. And it's a buffet, so if we're early, we get dibs."

I thought about how she'd tossed her dinner in the garbage last night. No wonder she was starving, especially after all that exercise. And I could wait to have breakfast with Sonnet, but knowing Sonnet, she'd be sleeping until the last possible second. Spider hadn't answered my text from last night, which meant he was sleeping too. Or shampooing. And I couldn't go bang on his door, obviously.

Besides, it was just breakfast. No sense making a big deal about it. Or being rude.

I got in the elevator with Ava.

The Muffin

AT HOME BREAKFAST WAS ALWAYS Dad's leftover goodies from the bakery: muffins, breads, scones, sometimes his
own personal recipe for granola. I loved everything he baked,
I really did, but it was a treat to get something different. And
since breakfast at the hotel was buffet style, I heaped all sorts
of breakfasty items on my plate: scrambled eggs, bacon, hash
brown potatoes, waffles. Also a cinnamon-looking muffin,
so I could report back to Dad, whose first question when we
returned from anywhere was always: *How was the baking?*

Followed by questions about the ingredients, the crust, the portion size.

When I'd filled my plate, I joined Ava at the table she'd chosen. She was sitting in front of a container of vanilla yogurt and a small bowl of fruit salad.

"I thought you were hungry," I said.

Ava narrowed her eyes as she took a half teaspoon of yogurt. "You know, I'm sick of everyone commenting on my food all the time."

"Who's everyone?"

"Nadia, my mom. *Everyone.* I just have this stomach thing, okay?"

"Sure." I munched on some maple-flavored bacon. "What kind of stomach thing?"

She groaned. "It's really none of your business."

"No, actually, I think it is. If we're eating together."

"God, Tally. You really *have* to argue about everything!"

"True." I chewed a blob of scrambled egg. "That's why Ms. Jordan loves me so much."

Ava smiled at that. "She *does* think you're kind of annoying. So do a lot of other people, frankly."

"I'm shattered."

"Well, but you *should* care what people think about you.

It's immature *not* to, you know? And you should *also* care how you look, how you dress—"

"Hey, I care how I dress."

"Yeah, that's really obvious." She rolled her eyes.

"No, I do care," I protested. "I care passionately about *not* following some brainless fashion trend, or being 'appropriate,' or worrying about my body type—whatever *that's* supposed to mean, anyway. I care about being creative, having fun with my outfits, expressing myself—"

"You care about acting like rules don't apply to you, so that way nobody can judge you. On anything but math."

"What?" I said it so forcefully my chest bumped into the table, spilling some of my OJ. "Ava, for your information—"

"Because the truth is, you're scared of people's opinions, aren't you, Tally. Deep down. You tell yourself you aren't, you *act* like you aren't, but secretly you're terrified."

I put down my fork and stared at her. "Ava, where did you get that from?"

"Just from everything I know about you. And watching you up close since we got here. Stuff like how you look at yourself in the mirror, or *don't* look. And how you stop exercising the second I walk into the room. I used to think you were just self-conscious about your size. And when you said you were adopted, I thought: Okay, so maybe *that* explains why you always need attention. But now I've changed my mind."

I was barely breathing. "You have?"

She nodded. "You're afraid everyone will think you're weird. Because that's just how you *are*. So you act obnoxious and dress that way to give people a *specific reason*— Oh, hey, Mom's here." She waved at Mrs. Seeley, who was talking to a bonnet-wearing woman with a full-length apron.

By that time, about half our grade was in the Thomas Jefferson, and I even saw Sonnet standing over at the bagels with Haley and Nadia. But I couldn't think of a way to get up from this table, especially now that Mrs. Seeley had seen us.

The truth was, Ava's comment had me paralyzed. *All this time, she'd been spying on me?* I was horrified—although really, how was it worse than *me* spying on *her*?

And what she'd said about me just now: that I was basically some kind of fake. I told myself she was wrong; she was just being mean; she didn't even *know* me.

Except Ava was Miss Perfection. She never made mistakes. About anything.

"Hey, Tally." Ava leaned toward me. "You finishing that muffin?"

I blinked at the seven-eighths-eaten cinnamon muffin on my plate. "No. Why? You want it?"

Without replying, she snatched the muffin eighth and set it on a napkin in front of her.

"I thought you didn't eat carbs," I said.

"Sometimes I do. Hi, Mom," she said brightly, as Mrs. Seeley took a seat at our table.

On her plate was what looked like a big squashed marshmallow. I guess she saw me staring at it, because she explained that it was scrambled egg whites.

Then she pointed her chin in the direction of my bacon. "Tally, please don't take this the wrong way, dear, but you might want to think a bit about your diet."

"My diet?" I repeated. "But I'm not on one."

"I mean diet as in 'foods you eat.' You're putting a lot of junk into your body."

"Mom!" Ava scolded. "Don't say that to her!"

Mrs. Seeley kept on talking. "You have a very pretty face, Tally, and such gorgeous thick hair. But I'd love to see you take better care of yourself, maybe add a few nice outfits into your wardrobe. I could make some suggestions, if you like."

I almost choked. "That's very generous of you, but I have tons of things."

"It's not about quantity, dear." Mrs. Seeley took a bite of squashed marshmallow. "I'm speaking from personal experience: Women need to look their best if they want to succeed."

"What if they don't?"

"Don't want to *succeed*?" Her face looked like she'd swallowed a bug.

"Yeah," I said. "What if they just want to build hummingbird houses? Or play the drums all day? Or solve Sudoku puzzles? And what if they don't care *what* people think about their bodies? Or their clothes?"

"Then good luck to them. Because grown-ups need jobs, Tally, and it's a tough world out there." Mrs. Seeley raised her eyebrows at Ava. "Although a junk-food diet never stopped your *father*. He always ate whatever he wanted."

"Mom, don't use the past tense," Ava said. "Dad still eats food."

"I'm sure he does. Just not in *my* kitchen. But let's not get me started on that subject." Her phone made a noise. She read something, looked excited, typed something. Then she looked up. "Ava, darling, is that all you're having for breakfast?"

"No, I also had a huge muffin," Ava said, showing her

the muffin remains. "It was whole wheat. And it had nuts for protein. Anyway, it was so delicious I had to let Tally have a bite. Right, Tally?"

She wanted me to lie about the muffin? Why? I searched her face for a clue. Ava was smiling, but now her eyes were pleading: *Just do this for me. PLEASE?*

It was an expression I'd never seen on her before. At that moment, she wasn't Miss Perfection, fearless leader of clone-girls. She looked desperate, really.

And one thing she had wrong about me: I wasn't just Miss Math, or a big obnoxious fake. I also took care of people. Even if sometimes maybe I shouldn't.

"Oh yes, you definitely did," I said.

Before Mrs. Seeley could challenge either one of us, her phone rang. She jumped up and ran from the table.

I looked at Ava, expecting some sort of thank-you or acknowledgement that I'd lied for her, but she turned away and just started reading her phone.

Great News

AS SOON AS BREAKFAST WAS over, Ms. Jordan told us to gather in the Martha Washington conference room to go over the day's schedule. By then Spider had shown up in the Thomas Jefferson to grab a doughnut for breakfast, and his mouth smelled stale, as if he'd forgotten to brush his teeth. I grinned at him as he ate his doughnut in the crowded conference room, careful not to spill any crumbs on the red carpeting, which had a Washington-crossing-the-Delaware pattern.

"What?" he said.

I grinned. "Nothing. I'm just watching you destroy that thing."

"It's a good doughnut, but your dad's are better. Tell him I said so, okay?" He leaned closer to me, so I got another whiff of his stinky breath. "Oh yeah, some spy updates: Marco's feet smell really bad, and he spits in the sink. But he doesn't even turn on the tap, so his spit blob just sits there."

"Gross," I said, laughing.

"Also, he's constantly on the phone. In the *bathroom*."

No wonder Spider couldn't brush his teeth. "That's terrible! Do you tell him to get out?"

"It's not a problem, Tally."

"Well, sure it is, if you can't use the bathroom, Spider!"

"It's fine. I'm not complaining; I'm just telling you because it's interesting."

"What's interesting about it?"

"The fact that it's so private. And that he keeps saying, 'Don't cry.'"

"Yeah? Who's he talking to?"

"No idea. It's hard to hear very much with the door closed."

I had to admit this was *extremely* interesting—even though ever since I'd watched Ava exercising, I'd been feeling a little off about the spy game. And after hearing she'd been spying on *me* . . . well, the whole thing had gotten weird. Still, I definitely wanted to hear more about Marco.

But then Ms. Jordan held up a hand to quiet us.

"Okay, folks, so there's some good news and some great news," she said. "The good news is that this afternoon, we're doing the US Capitol, followed by a tour of the Mint. The great news . . ." She smiled, a bit nervously, I thought. "Ava's mom, Mrs. Seeley, has just now arranged a very special backstage tour of the Kennedy Center."

Haley gasped. "Omigod. *Omigod.* Ms. Jordan, isn't that where they're doing—"

"Yes, the national touring company of *Hamilton* is in town, and they're doing some performances at the Kennedy Center this week. We tried to get tickets, but I'm afraid it's just not possible—"

Haley and all the other theater-and-music kids screamed. So did Sonnet, who was with them. Even though Ms. Jordan had just said she *hadn't* gotten tickets. It was crazy.

And Mrs. Seeley was beaming proudly. "Yes, I'm just delighted! The assistant stage manager at the Kennedy Center happens to be my old college roommate Sarah, and now she's a client of mine. So when she heard about our trip, she graciously offered to meet us and take us around a bit, but she wasn't sure until just this morning that it could be arranged. And during breakfast, she called to say we were on!"

So that was the exciting phone call. I wondered if Ava knew what her mom had been busy arranging. She sure didn't give very much away, did she?

"Will we see actual performers rehearsing?" Haley squealed. "Or get to meet anyone backstage?"

"No guarantees, but you never know," Mrs. Seeley answered. She fluttered her eyelashes in a teasing way.

More screams. Across the room, Sonnet was hopping, first on one foot, then the other, as if the floor were giving her small electric shocks.

Then Ms. Jordan made *settle down* hands. "But here's the catch: Only thirty of us are allowed. They're very strict on the number of guests backstage, so we're asking those of you who aren't super interested, or who don't do music and theater at school, to please raise your hands. We'd like to give dibs on the Kennedy Center to classmates with the strongest interest in the performing arts."

"That's so unfair," Sydney Brunner grumbled. "Just

because I don't play an an-stru-mant, I don't see why I should be pun-ashed."

"No one's being punished, Sydney," Mr. G said cheerfully. "We'll have an alternate activity for you guys, extremely cool, so no worries."

Sydney sniffed the air suspiciously. "What is it?"

"Well, that's the beauty of plan B: It's entirely up to us."

At first nobody raised any hands. Then Spider raised his.

"What are you doing?" I whispered at him.

"Telling the truth," he said, shrugging.

"But you do music! You play trumpet!"

"Yeah, but it's not like I *care* about it."

My heart sank. Because who asked Spider to tell the truth? If he wasn't going to the Kennedy Center, naturally I wasn't going either.

Reluctantly, I raised my hand.

Other people raised theirs, too: Sydney, then Jamal, then Shanaya, then Marco. Plus a bunch of kids from Mr. G's class.

But not Sonnet, of course. She was huddled in the corner with Haley, Nadia, and some other theater people. Her back was turned, so I couldn't see her face or make eye contact. But I could see she was wearing her hair unponytailed and parted on the side, the clonegirl way. Rooming with Haley had given her a new hairstyle, apparently. Maybe hairstyles were contagious, like cold germs or pinkeye.

"Thank you, volunteers," Mr. G was saying. "But we still need a few more of you for plan B, or we'll have to start picking names out of a hat. Come on, we'll have a blast, and I know some great spots for lunch. Hey, that's awesome."

He was smiling at Ava, who was now waving her arm over her head, like a flag.

"Ava, what are you *doing*?" Nadia shrieked.

"I've been to the Kennedy Center before," Ava replied. "And backstage once. And I've already seen *Hamilton*. So I'm totally fine with plan B."

I glanced at Mrs. Seeley, who seemed to have something stuck in her throat. "Ava, darling," she said, and she did a pretend chuckle. "That's really generous of you, but since you're my daughter, and this tour was arranged as a thank-you to *me*, I think we can make an exception—"

"No, Mom, it's fine," Ava answered firmly. "It wouldn't be fair if I went today. Other kids should get a chance."

"Are you sure?" Ms. Jordan asked. Her eyes flitted to Mrs. Seeley's face, I saw.

"Completely." Ava was using her quiet voice, which was somehow more forceful than her loud one.

And for the second time in the space of an hour, I wondered what the bleep was going on in her mind. She sure wasn't staying off the tour for social reasons, because all her friends, except for Sydney and Shanaya, were going. And it wasn't like she wanted to hang out with *me*; I had no illusions about *that*.

I watched as Mrs. Seeley pushed herself over to where Ava was standing and begin to argue with her—quietly, but with a lot of gestures. They were too far away for me to hear anything, but I could tell that Mrs. Seeley was frustrated with how Ava just kept shaking her head. And then I had a strange thought: Whatever they were arguing about, it had nothing to do with the Kennedy Center.

Superhero Dolphin

"TALLY?" NOW SONNET WAS IN front of Spider and me, with Haley right behind her. "I feel terrible you guys aren't going."

"It's fine," I said, chewing my lower lip.

"Tally, you don't have to stay behind because of me," Spider said.

"I'm not," I lied.

"So why are you doing it, then?"

"Why? Because plan B sounds mysterious, and you know how I love mysteries."

Sonnet and Haley exchanged glances.

"Tally, can I talk to you a sec?" Sonnet asked.

Without waiting for me to answer, she dragged me over to the wall, next to a portrait of Martha Washington. "Spider doesn't need a babysitter," she announced.

"What?" I stared at her. Not only was her hair different, she wasn't wearing her small gold heart studs anymore, either. The earrings she had on were big silver hoops. "Sonnet, I'm not—"

"Exactly. You *aren't* his babysitter, but sometimes you act like you are, and that's not being fair to him. Or to you."

"That's crazy," I sputtered. "Did Haley tell you that?"

"You think I can't see things for myself?" Sonnet raised her chin. "And as long as we're on the subject, Tally, you do the same thing to me."

"*Excuse* me?"

"Well, it's true. Sometimes you act like Spider and I can't take care of ourselves. It's like you think we're these drowning swimmers, and you're this superhero dolphin who can save us."

"*Superhero dolphin?*" I gaped at her. It definitely sounded like a line she'd heard from Haley, or maybe even Nadia. "Sonnet, what are you *talking* about?"

"I mean, seriously, Tally, I'm really grateful for the way you stopped the teasing after my audition. And the way you made me feel better about the whole thing afterward. You helped me *a lot* back when I first moved here, you know? But I'm not the scared new kid anymore, so you can please *stop* now."

I was buzzing like a nearly dead lightbulb. "Well, I'm really sorry, okay? I never meant to—"

"I've been thinking this for a while, actually," Sonnet continued, her cheeks bright pink. "And you know what? I think Spider feels the same way. I think he's getting tired of how you treat him."

Now my throat ached. Sonnet had been thinking this *for a while*? Since when? Probably before we got on the bus, or even before that. I tried to scroll back in time to a point when Sonnet had seemed happy that we were friends, but my brain had crashed.

She seemed to realize that she'd hurt my feelings. "Tally, look, you're a really good person . . . ," she began.

I knew what word came next: *But*. Well, I didn't want to hear it.

"Sonnet," I said loudly, "for your information, I just want to be *with* Spider, not babysit *for* him. Maybe you don't believe it; maybe Haley doesn't either. But it's the truth. Okay?"

She shrugged. "Okay."

"And I don't think I'm some kind of rescue dolphin, or whatever you said. I'm really glad you're doing better now. Oh, and I like your hair. And those earrings."

Sonnet fingered the silver hoops. "Thank you, Tally. Haley let me borrow them, so."

"I figured. Well, that was extremely nice of her."

At that point I knew she wanted me to tell her, *Have fun backstage; take a selfie with the Schuyler sisters; get some autographs*—but I refused. I was being a loyal friend to Spider. If Sonnet wanted to spend the afternoon with clonegirls, that was her business.

And as I watched her walk back over to Haley, I wondered if this was the last conversation we'd ever have. It kind of felt that way, like if this were a movie, the camera would be pulling away, and pretty soon all you'd see would be a big empty highway.

"Okay," Mr. G was saying in a fun-counselor sort of voice. "All you non-theatrical types, follow Mrs. Packer, Mr. Melton and me."

They led us to the lobby, where Roy took off his three-cornered hat and bowed at us. I took off my green glasses and bowed back, but apparently he didn't notice.

"So what's plan B?" Marco asked skeptically. Trey had deserted him for the Kennedy Center, and it was obvious he was disappointed. Some people were just sucky friends, when it came down to it, and I almost told Marco I knew how he felt.

"Plan B," Mr. G said, "will be decided by popular vote. We have several great possibilities. We could do the Museum of Natural History—"

"Bor-ang," said Sydney.

"—or the National Gallery of Art—"

"Nah," Marco said.

Then it hit me.

"Wait, what about the Air and Space Museum?" I cried.

Spider's eyes lit up and he started bouncing on the balls of his feet. "Yeah, Mr. G, *could* we?"

"They have a museum for *space*?" Marco asked, laughing. "So you mean it's completely empty? Except for the black holes?"

"Marco, it's actually incredible," I said, catching Spider's eye. "Just look it up online!"

While everyone read their phones, I told myself that if we *were* doing Air and Space, I didn't mind missing plan A.

I mean, just to see the look on Spider's face right then, like it was Christmas morning on the moon, was worth everything about this trip, even having to room with Ava.

"Okay," Marco said after a minute. "I agree with Tally—it does look amazing. Let's do it, Mr. G!"

Spider grinned at me.

Mr. G held up his hand. "First we need to take a vote: How many in favor of checking out Air and Space?"

Everyone raised their hands, including Ava.

"The popular vote is unanimous," Mr. G said, rubbing his hands together. "And may I commend you on an awesome choice. All right, people, *vámanos*."

Popcorn

WAY, WAY BACK IN THE olden days before the bakery opened and Dad was just messing around in the kitchen, he tried to get me interested in baking. Specifically, he tried to teach me how to bake bread. But I thought bread baking was boring: all that kneading, and then just sitting around watching a blob of dough for hours and hours. The only type of cooking I enjoyed was making popcorn, because it was exciting—like a food explosion, I told him. One minute you had a corn kernel, and then suddenly, *pop*. It was something different.

Although Dad said, "Yes, Tally, you're right, making

popcorn *is* like an explosion. But it's also a whole process. First you add oil to the pan, and heat. The kernels turn from brown to yellow, and get fatter and rounder. Then they start sputtering and hopping in the pan. And when they get so hot they can't stand it anymore, they pop. So really, if you think about it, it's no different from making bread."

"No, Daddy, it's the *opposite* of bread," I insisted. "Popcorn is *fast*." I clapped my hands once, to show him how fast it seemed to me.

Dad smiled. "What I'm saying is, if you know how to look at it, you'll see that popcorn doesn't happen all at once. It's faster than baking bread, sure, but it still happens step by step."

At the time, I had no idea what he was talking about. How was baking bread the same as making popcorn? It wasn't. One took forever; the other didn't. I had no patience for anything that made you wait, so after that, every time Dad preheated the oven, I managed to slip away from the kitchen. Pretty soon Dad got the message that I wasn't a baker and had zero interest in anything but the eating part.

I never thought about this conversation, which had happened approximately one million years ago. But that morning at the Air and Space Museum, I remembered what Dad had said about making popcorn—how it *seemed* like a sudden explosion but really wasn't. What made me think about this was watching Spider. As soon as we entered the museum and bought our tickets, he transformed: *pop*. Out on the street, he was quiet and nervous, the way he always was; inside the museum, it was as if he'd spontaneously combusted. He ran upstairs ahead of everybody into the Apollo room and began explaining everything there in a loud, enthusiastic voice: The Skylab 4 command module. The lunar roving vehicle. The F-1 engine.

"Dude, you're like some NASA supergeek," Marco told him. "How do you know so much about this?"

Spider beamed. "I just read a lot."

"Yeah, but how do you remember all those details?" It was like Marco wondered if Spider had a secret method he could share with him. Like he wished he could be as smart as Spider. Where had this come from all of a sudden? It was weird.

"I have a cool book I brought for the bus ride," Spider told him. "When we get back to the room, I could show it to you."

"Awesome," Marco said, grinning. "Hey, you know how this thing works?" He pointed to some control-panel thing in the Skylab 4.

And Spider said some theories about what it could be for. What was going on here? Had Spider undergone some kind of secret personality transplant? Of course not, I scolded myself.

But if he hadn't changed suddenly, dramatically, like a kernel of corn in a hot frying pan, had he been changing all along . . . and I hadn't noticed?

And Marco also, for that matter? That could explain the strange phone call Spider had heard in the bathroom. Well, not explain it—just explain how Marco could care that someone was crying. Whoever it was.

And why he was being so nice to Spider. Which I had to admit he was.

"Isn't it incredible?" Mr. G was by my side as we headed to the next room to see the 1903 Wright Flyer. But I couldn't tell what, exactly, he was referring to—the exhibit, the whole museum, or Spider's behavior. So I just made a "yeah" sort of sound.

Then I heard my voice ask: "Mr. G, why do people get obsessed with things?"

"Good question," Mr. G said. "But you tell me, Tally. You're obsessed with math, aren't you?"

"Me?" I looked at him. He wasn't even my teacher; how

much did he know about me, anyway? "I'm not *obsessed* with it. I just like it."

"Fair enough. But why?"

He couldn't possibly be talking about Marisa or Bio-dad. So maybe he was asking about all the unknown variables in the Me equation. "I don't know! It's just how my brain works."

"Yeah, well, I'm guessing it's the same with any obsession. You develop an interest in things that click with your particular way of thinking. And *why* your brain works that way, who knows. Could be genetic, could be environment, very likely a combination of the two. Anyway, it looks to me like your friend has found his subject." He looked over at Spider, who was telling Marco something about the Wright brothers.

"Nah," I said. "Spider's interested in a lot of things. He flips around all the time."

"Until he finds a subject that's his subject, with a capital S. And then, watch out, world."

Mr. G smiled and walked over to Sydney and Shanaya. His smile annoyed me. It was the same sort of smile as the one he'd given me at the Vietnam Memorial—and it was like he was implying we both knew something, even agreed about something, when it came to Spider. But what, exactly, were we agreeing about? And how could he—Spider's teacher for just a few weeks at the start of the school year—know my best friend as well as I did?

Although, how well did I know Spider, really? I mean, he was choosing Marco over me, at least right now, here in this museum. Maybe Sonnet was right about the way Spider felt; maybe he really did think I treated him like a baby.

And wished I hadn't come here. So he could have time with Marco by himself.

The thought kicked me in the stomach.

Ugh.

How come I didn't see all that before?

I'm an idiot. A total, massively idiotic—

"So you like this place?" Now Ava had wandered over to me.

"Yeah, it's really fascinating," I said. "Don't you think so?"

"Not especially. I get bored fast in museums."

"Then why'd you vote to come here?"

Ava shrugged. "Everyone else wanted to come. And I didn't care one way or the other."

I looked at her. Maybe that beige sweater did wash her

out; her skin looked like uncooked oatmeal. "So what *do* you care about?"

"Me?" She grabbed her hair in a ponytail. Then she opened her hand, and the ponytail went free. "If I tell you, you'll just make some snotty comment."

"No, I won't, Ava. I promise."

"Okay, fine." She looked at me through her pale eyelashes. "You know those magazines in our room? I care about those."

I stared. "You mean those fashion ones? *Why?*"

"Because the articles are really smart and funny. And my dream job is to write for them someday."

"Cool," I said, because it seemed like the thing to say.

"I'm not a math nerd like you, Tally. I'm a fashion nerd. And I refuse to hear you say anything negative about that."

"Well, I'm not, okay? I just didn't know that about you."

"Right. And now you do."

We didn't say anything for a few seconds. It was awkward, but not in a bad way.

Then I heard my voice. "Can I ask you a question, Ava? How come you didn't go on the Kennedy Center tour?"

"I told you. I've been there already."

"But just on the general tour, right? This one was *special.*"

"Yes, maybe, but it's still just a bunch of dressing rooms."

"Although they *might* meet the cast of *Hamilton*, which would be pretty amazing. Considering how everyone is so obsessed with that show—"

"Yeah, well. Mom wasn't promising anything."

I saw Spider bouncing on his toes as he talked to Marco. Marco said something, and then Spider did his laugh, the one with the *hyuk-hyuk* sound. It was hard to watch, so I turned away.

And I'm not sure how it happened, or why, but all of a sudden I was asking Ava if she wished her mom hadn't come on the trip.

Ava's eyebrows met. "Are you *saying* something, Tally?"

"Not really."

"Okay. Good."

But it was so strange how I couldn't shut up. "Is that why you didn't go to the Kennedy Center? So you could be on your own? For the day, I mean?"

She looked shocked.

My mouth kept moving. "Because your mom is, like, *really intense*. So if you needed time away from her . . ."

"Who says I did?"

"It wouldn't be surprising." I shrugged. "My mom's

kind of the opposite. So is my dad. I mean, I know I'm incredibly lucky. But I bet it's hard for you dealing with your mom about everything."

Now Ava's eyes were like slits. "Tally, that's really insulting," she said. "To my mom."

"Sorry! I just meant that *if* you felt that way, I *completely understand—*"

"You don't understand *anything*," Ava snapped, and stomped off.

Pythagoras

WE STAYED AT THE MUSEUM for three hours. The whole time, Spider and Marco kept talking together, walking a few feet in front of me, not looking back. But once, I heard Marco call him Astro Boy—which struck me as a compliment nickname, like Math Girl.

Don't think I wasn't glad for Spider, by the way. I was. The fact that his former bully wasn't just an okay roommate but actually, at this moment, an *almost friend* made me feel relieved—but also, I have to admit, kind of shaky. It wasn't that I was jealous; it was more that I didn't know what to do with myself. My whole life I'd taken care of Spider, and now it felt like he'd shoved me out of the sandbox. Which I knew wasn't true, of course: Just because he'd been ignoring me all morning didn't mean the two of us weren't still friends. But something had changed—maybe for good—between us. And I couldn't help wondering if it was my fault, for not seeing things better. Especially something other people had noticed first.

At noon, Mr. G announced that the next stop was lunch. He gave us a choice of restaurants: a pizza place, a burger place, or a Thai place. Marco said he was voting for Thai food, and it surprised me when Spider, an incredibly picky eater, agreed. Shanaya, Sydney, Jamal, and I all wanted pizza, so Mr. G put the question to a vote. The Thai place won, only because Ava switched her vote at the last minute.

We got to the restaurant at twelve thirty. Spider was still blabbing about the lunar rover, and Marco seemed to be paying attention. Still.

"Mr. G, I don't know what to order," Shanaya announced, as we all stared at our menus.

"What say we order a bunch of dishes for the table," Mr. G suggested. "That way you folks can sample different things and see what you like."

"Awesome," Marco said. "That's what my dad always used to do."

"*Used* to?" I asked.

"Yeah. Before he moved out last year."

"I never even had a dad," Spider blurted.

"How is that possible?" Althea Packer teased.

"I just mean, no one I've ever met." Spider's lip quivered a micromillimeter.

I knew that lip quiver; I'd spent years being on the watch for it. Before I could stop myself, I jumped in.

"You want to hear something crazy I just found out?" I said. "It's about Pythagoras."

"Who?" Sydney said.

"You know, the ancient Greek mathematician. The guy who figured out about right triangles—a squared plus b squared equals c squared. Well, I read this article that said he was deathly afraid of beans."

"*Beans?*" Jamal said, laughing.

"Yeah, especially fava beans. He thought they contained the souls of the dead, so if you ate beans it was like you were eating your ancestors."

"Haha, yeah, because *human beans*," Marco said.

"Oh, and every time you farted, he thought you were losing part of your soul."

Everyone was staring at me. Mr. G stroked his beard, like he didn't know what else to do.

"I swear," I added. "You can look it up."

"Tally," Shanaya said. "Why *exactly* are you saying all this? We were just having a serious conversation."

"Yeah, I know. So I thought I'd liven it up a little."

"By mentioning bean farts? And ancient Greek math guys?" Shanaya shook her long twists.

"Sometimes things just pop into my head."

"Well, you should try listening to *other people*, you know?" She whispered something to Sydney, who rolled her eyes and nodded.

The waiter came to take Mr. G's order. I personally loved Thai food, especially anything spicy, with noodles—but hearing all the dishes Mr. G was ordering, I wondered if Spider would find something to eat. Other than chili dogs, he never ate spicy food, and he wasn't big on trying new stuff in general.

While we were waiting for the food, Mr. G and Mr. Melton started talking about some local baseball team with the hilarious name the Washington Gnats. I tried to catch Spider's eye so we could share a laugh about it (*haha, the Minneapolis Stinkbugs, the Boston Ticks, the Los Angeles Lice*), but he wasn't ever looking in my direction. He just kept nodding and smiling whenever Marco mentioned some meaningless baseball statistic, as if he even knew what Marco was talking about, which he didn't.

And I thought: *Okay, Spider, so you have a new friend; but you don't need to* lie *to him, do you?*

When the food finally arrived, Mr. G told us to help ourselves, and if we couldn't reach a dish we wanted, to just pass our plate. Right away, all sixteen kids (plus three grownups) started passing our plates counterclockwise, ending up with food we couldn't identify. I waited for Spider's reaction to the Mystery Food in front of him, but he just picked up his pair of chopsticks (*when did he learn to use chopsticks?*) and began eating some noodles.

So I ate too. The food was pretty good, but I barely tasted anything.

Finally I got tired of stuffing things into my mouth, and looked up. Mrs. Packer and Mr. G were talking about car problems. Althea was talking to Drake about some Netflix series I didn't watch. Sad-nay was telling Shanaya about a fight she'd had with her mom. Jamal and Damon were arguing about some football statistic. Sammie, Desiree, and Annie were discussing a party I hadn't been invited to.

E pluribus unum, I thought. *Ha.* We were the same as back at Eastview, only with chopsticks.

Oh, but also one other difference: Now I was on my own, without Spider or Sonnet.

At the far end of the table, Ava was sitting next to a boy named Javier. They weren't talking to each other, though. She was moving things around her plate with her chopsticks, looking busy and organized, typing into her phone with her free hand. But if you looked closely, which I did, you could see that her food was all on her plate, uneaten.

Us-ies

AFTER LUNCH WE WENT TO the Capitol building, where we met the Kennedy Center kids, who wouldn't shut up. They'd been in a dressing room and the rehearsal studio; they'd seen the costume shop; they'd met the choreographer. They'd even waved at some *Hamilton* chorus members, who'd waved back. Woo-hoo.

Mrs. Seeley, of course, was glowing. "I'm so *thrilled* I was able to arrange this for us! I know you'll all remember this day forever!" she gushed. And she made all the kids promise to send personal thank-yous to her college friend, who was kind enough to blahblahblah.

"Well, *we* had a great morning too," Mr. G said. He grinned at the plan B people.

"Actually, we did," Marco said. He didn't even sound sarcastic.

Sonnet insisted on showing me selfies. Except they weren't selfies; they were *us*-ies. *Here* we *are in the dressing room. Here* we *are in the hallway.* Every photo was about Sonnet and Haley, or Sonnet and Nadia, or Sonnet, Haley, and Nadia. I just stood there like an idiot while she showed them all to me in chronological order, going "Huh," "Wow," and "Nice shot."

Then they ran over to Ava to show her all the photos. While Ava was surrounded, Mrs. Seeley came over to me.

"Oh, Tally," she said. "I'm so sorry you couldn't join us. The tour was truly a once-in-a-lifetime experience."

"Yeah, I'm sure it was," I said, looking past her to where Marco and Spider were now chatting with Trey. Who was laughing. About what?

"Did you enjoy yourself at the Air and Space Museum?"

"Me? Oh, definitely."

"And I hear that afterward you had lunch at a nice restaurant?"

"Uh-huh. Thai food." Why was Marco resting his elbow

on Spider's shoulder? Was Spider okay with it? He wasn't protesting, but that didn't mean he *liked* it.

"Everyone enjoyed the food? Including Ava?"

"What?" Slowly Mrs. Seeley came into focus. "I'm sorry?"

She smiled, but there was something twitchy about her mouth. "Ava enjoyed the food?"

Finally I got it: She was asking me to report on Ava's food intake.

And for a second I panicked, because I wasn't sure what to say. If I lied, I'd be protecting Ava from her mother, but I wouldn't be helping her, really. If I told Mrs. Seeley the truth, Ava would kill me; and I had no idea how her mom would react, anyway. Maybe she'd blast me for telling her something she didn't want to hear: *Dear Mrs. Seeley, Your daughter isn't perfect. She's pretty messed up, to be totally honest with you. Sincerely, Talia Martin.*

So I pretended to think for a minute. "I'm not sure. We weren't sitting together. I think she ordered chicken pad thai?"

"Yum!" Mrs. Seeley exclaimed, and right away I could tell I'd made the right choice. Mrs. Seeley had heard me say that Ava had *eaten* the pad thai; maybe that was all she'd wanted to hear.

I let her pat my shoulder.

"Well, I'm so excited about the Capitol tour," she gushed. "Aren't you?"

Before I could answer, she was at Ava's side again, oohing over the photos.

That afternoon we did the Capitol building and the US Mint. The whole time, Spider kept running back and forth between Marco and me. And Sonnet kept on trying to include me in her new circle, which consisted of Haley, Nadia, Shanaya, and Sydney. Oh, and sometimes Ava, except when Mrs. Seeley insisted on talking to her daughter.

But the thing was, I had no interest in being a clonegirl. So whenever Sonnet tried to sweep me into their formation, I hung back to retie my sneakers.

One time when I was pretend-double-knotting my laces, Marco came over.

"Hey," he said.

I got up and waited, but he didn't add anything. He just stood there looking at me from under his eyelashes. All of a sudden I realized that we were the same height. And this was strange, because we'd never been before.

"Can I ask you a question, Marco?" I blurted. "Why are you being so nice to Spider?"

He looked confused. "I shouldn't be nice to him?"

"I just mean you were horrible to him last year. Don't you remember?"

He rubbed his cheek. "No, of course I do. I was a total jerk, and so was Trey. But that was back when we were *all* being stupid—"

"Not everyone, Marco. *I* wasn't. And I don't get why you're his friend *now.*"

"I don't know," Marco said slowly, as if he was figuring it out for the first time. "I just think he's really smart. He was always so quiet, and I think he hid behind you a lot, so I guess I never noticed it before. Anyway, people change. Don't you think *you* have?"

Me? But we weren't talking about me. And anyway, how could you *know* if you had changed, in a way that meant something real about you as a person? It wasn't like watching yourself do jumping jacks in the mirror: You couldn't see your own feelings jiggle.

Although possibly you watched your feelings bounce off other people, or something.

And as I watched Marco walk over to Spider, I could tell my feelings were bouncing off him at that exact moment.

The Shovel

AT SIX THIRTY, WE HEADED back to the hotel for dinner. The last thing I wanted was a meal with Sonnet and the clonegirls, or with Ava and her mom, so I sat at Mr. G's table with Spider, Marco, and Trey. They were still discussing baseball—and now Mr. G was talking about getting tickets to see the Gnats play.

"You mean tonight?" Marco asked excitedly. His eyes lit up.

"Sure, why not?" Mr. G replied. "*If* we can get tickets. I'm thinking maybe some of you guys who didn't get to go to the Kennedy Center deserve a special treat."

"Trey did the Kennedy Center," Marco reminded him.

"Yeah, well, plan B kids get dibs," Mr. G replied. "Trey can go if there's room."

"That's fair," Trey admitted, which kind of surprised me.

Then Mr. G went around the restaurant to ask which Eastview kids wanted to come to the baseball game (*if* he could get tickets, he kept adding). When he returned to our table he reported that twenty-seven kids wanted to see the Gnats.

"Plus you four, plus Mr. Melton and Mrs. Gilroy, equals thirty-four tickets all together," Mr. G said, typing into his phone. "*If* we can get that many tickets, which is a big question, they're going to be way up in the bleachers."

"Wait," I said. "Don't include me, Mr. G." I tried to catch Spider's eye, but he pretended to be fascinated by the mustard on his hot dog.

"Ah, too bad," Mr. G said. "You sure, Tally?"

"Yeah, baseball puts me in a coma." I swallowed. "And besides, I'm really not . . . feeling so well."

"Tally, you're sick?" Spider asked, looking at me, finally.

"Kind of." I put down my fork.

"Well, Ms. Jordan says that kids who aren't going can watch a movie at the hotel. Let me talk to her." He left the table again.

"What's wrong with you, Tally? You got your period?" Trey sniggered.

"Shut up, Trey," Marco snapped. "That's not even funny."

Hearing Marco stick up for me made my heart skitter. So that I wouldn't have to look at him, I glared at Trey. "I'd just rather not go to some boring baseball game," I told him. "Is that so incomprehensible, you microbe?"

"Whatever." Trey took a ketchupy bite of burger.

Spider was watching me with worried eyes. "Can I talk to you, Tally? In private?"

"Absolutely."

We got up from the table and walked into the lobby, where Roy, Hipster Bonnet, and some other people were doing a minuet while some guy in a vest and knee socks played a fiddle.

"Do you want me to stay here with you?" Spider asked. "Because I will."

That was so sweet. Immediately I forgave him for how he'd ignored me the whole time at the Air and Space Museum. And at the Thai restaurant at lunch. And also just now at dinner.

"Only if you'd rather not go to this stupid baseball game," I said.

He shrugged.

Then I thought about what Sonnet had said, how Spider was sick of me acting like his babysitter. So I added quickly: "You know, I don't *expect* you to do anything. I mean, it's totally your decision."

"Yeah, I know." He stuck his hands in his pockets and stared at the dancers. "Well, as long as you don't need me here, I guess I'll go to the game."

Wait, what? He wasn't supposed to say that.

I stared at him. "Spider, you *detest* baseball."

"No," he said, blinking. "I used to."

"What does that mean?"

"I don't know. I think I changed my opinion."

"Seriously? You're standing here telling me that all of a sudden, now you *actually like*—"

"Tally, you're shouting."

"Sorry." I took a breath. "This is really about hanging out with Marco, right? Why can't you be honest and just admit it?"

Spider's eyes flashed. "Tally, are you accusing me of *lying* to you?"

"No. Not exactly."

"Yeah, you are. First about liking baseball, then about

Marco. And I've never lied to you about *anything*. In my whole *life*."

"I know that," I admitted.

His breathing was getting fast. "So I'm *really mad* at you for saying that just now."

Hipster Bonnet made a *shh* finger at us.

"Sorry," I said quickly. "Please calm down, Spider, okay?"

His face was red. "Don't tell me what to do!"

"I'm not! I just don't want you to lose it, all right? In *public*."

"You're telling me to calm down, which is a *thing* to *do*. I'm really *sick* of it, Tally, you know that? And I wish you were happy I'd made a new friend!" Spider was shouting even louder than before.

The minuet stopped. Now Hipster Bonnet and Roy were looking alarmed, whispering to each other, probably wondering if they should call the Minutemen. Or maybe a teacher or somebody.

And then Derrick and Jamal walked out of the Thomas Jefferson, followed by Shanaya and Sydney.

I tried to ignore them. "Believe me, I *am* happy for you," I whispered fiercely. "I just wish you could be *yourself* with Marco, not pretend to be interested in something you actually *hate*."

"Tally, we're not in the sandbox anymore! *I don't need you to protect my shovel.*"

Shanaya giggled behind her hands. "Protect my shovel" must have sounded kind of crazy, even without the shouting, but it wasn't like I could start explaining.

For an endless minute, Spider and I stared at each other. It was like I was watching a storm cloud pass in slow motion—as the seconds went by, I could tell he wasn't going to fall apart, or have a panic attack, or have trouble breathing. But he was still furious at me. And I wanted to defend myself, but I had no idea how. Especially in the hotel lobby, with all these other people standing there, watching.

Finally he shook his head. "Can I tell you something, Tally? Every day you come to school looking completely different—weird clothes, and all that other crazy stuff you put on. But it's like no one *else* gets to change *anything*. Ever."

"What? What are you talking about?" My voice sounded strange. Really, it didn't even sound like my own voice. "That doesn't even make any—"

"Marco is nice, okay? And I like baseball. Or, at least, I'm willing to give it a try. Why can't you deal with that?"

"Fine. Go ahead," I snapped. "Does Marco know you're

completely ignorant about the game? Or maybe you lied to him about that fact too? So that he wouldn't think you're weird?"

As soon as I said this, I thought: *Bleep. How could you say something so mean to Spider, of all people? What's going on with you, Tally?*

Although Spider didn't even answer the question. He just crossed his arms on his chest like he was protecting himself from me, or maybe making a decision.

"I hope you feel better, Tally," he said quietly, and walked back into the restaurant.

Black Hole

AFTER THE WAY I'D JUST screwed up with Spider, I couldn't face going back to the restaurant. So for a while I just sat in the lobby, waiting for Sonnet to finish supper. I knew she was at the clonegirl table—but there was an atom of a possibility that she'd walk out of the Thomas Jefferson on her own. She didn't, of course, but she did exit with only Haley, so I felt okay about pouncing.

"Hey, Sonnet, could I talk to you a minute?" I asked.

She checked with Haley; I saw it.

"No problem," Haley answered. "I'll see you upstairs, Sonnet."

We watched Haley get into the elevator and wave at us in a *bye-bye* sort of way.

"So," I said to Sonnet. "I feel like I haven't seen you all day!"

"Just in the morning," Sonnet replied. "And frankly, Tally, every time I tried to talk to you this afternoon, you walked away."

"That's because you were hanging out with clonegirls!"

"I wish you wouldn't call them that word. It's actually kind of mean. And they're all very nice, once you get to know them." Her brow puckered. "Especially Haley. We've been singing *Hamilton* together in the bathroom."

"Why the bathroom?" I didn't care; it was just a way to change the subject.

But Sonnet took the question seriously. "Acoustics. And she's been coaching me about my stage fright. She knows all these cool relaxation techniques."

"Cool," I said super enthusiastically.

"She says I have a really good voice."

"Because you do! Haven't I told you that a million times?"

"Yeah. But Haley's always the lead in everything. So

coming from her, you know? It means a lot." She turned pink. "She wants me to audition again. She says she'll help me rehearse."

And therefore I'm losing Sonnet for good, I thought. *Well, it was probably inevitable.*

"What about the moose?" I asked, trying to sound playful.

"The what?"

"That pink stuffed animal you were spying on, remember? So does Haley sleep with it?" I made my face look interested.

"I forgot to check. But it's really cute, so I wouldn't be surprised." Sonnet glanced at her phone. "Tally, we should go change now."

"For what?"

"The baseball game. Mr. G just said he got the tickets." She glanced at my bowling shirt. "You're going to the game, right?"

"Actually, no," I said. "I'm staying here."

"At the hotel? What for?"

"To wash my hair."

"You're joking."

"I never joke. I'm an extremely serious person, as you know."

Sonnet didn't even smile at that. "Well, I wish you were coming with us." She paused. "I also wish you sat with us at supper."

Us. As if Haley and Nadia and all those other girls wanted me to join them.

"I'll definitely sit with you guys for breakfast," I lied. "Anyway, have fun tonight! Go, Bugs!"

She gave me a funny look, then a speed hug, then ran into the open elevator.

I counted to sixty for her to get into her room, then took the stairs back to Lexington 06. As soon as I was inside our room, I spied a plastic container of uneaten food on the dresser and heard the sound of water in the bathroom.

I flopped on my bed. Was this the worst day of my life? Possibly it was. Anyway, as I stared at the battle pattern on my comforter, I couldn't think of a worse one.

"Hey," Ava said as she came out of the bathroom. "Going to that baseball game?"

"Nope," I said.

She gave me a look. "How come? Aren't your friends going?"

I shrugged.

"Oh, I get it. It's weird for you that they have new friends, right?"

I decided not to respond. But it shocked me that she'd

picked up on this. Obviously, she'd been spying more than I'd realized.

I watched nervously as she opened her drawer and pulled out the pink tank I'd tried on. She went into the bathroom to put it on. A minute later she came out wearing her bathrobe and tossed the tank into the trash.

My heart pounded. Why didn't she want it anymore? Had I stretched it out? I couldn't have; the material was superhero stretchy. Maybe she'd decided she was anti-pink.

I watched her take off her bathrobe. Underneath was a clingy blue T-shirt. How come she wore clothes that showed (almost) how skinny she was? You'd think she'd be embarrassed.

"So are *you* going to the game?" I asked, trying to sound casual.

Ava shook her head. "No, I'd rather work out in the gym tonight. Afterward I'll probably go to that movie they're showing downstairs. And Mom will be here, so."

As she bent over to tie her sneaker laces, I could count every bone in her spine through the T-shirt.

And once again I couldn't stop myself. "Ava, can I please say something?"

"Maybe." She kept tying. "What about?"

"You," I blurted. "You aren't eating. I see you brought a doggy bag back from supper just now, and you didn't eat any lunch at the Thai place. And at breakfast you made me lie to your mom about that muffin—"

She sat up. "For your information, I eat a perfectly healthy diet. Lots of fruits and vegetables. And protein—"

"But no actual calories."

Her face was red. "Tally, what I eat has nothing to do with *you*, all right?"

"But it's *not* all right, that's the thing. I don't think you're healthy. You *look* bad."

Her eyes widened. "Oh, and I suppose you think you look so cool in that ridiculous bowling shirt with those stupid glasses—"

"I told you I think they're funny. And I'm not hurting myself by wearing them."

She grabbed her hair and made a ponytail, this time with an actual rubber band. "Well, thanks for being so nosy, but I'm fine."

"I don't think you are, though." I swallowed. "I think something may be wrong. I mean, with *you*."

Ava stared at me. Her chin trembled, as if she was fighting tears.

"Tally, I know you're smart," she said, and now her voice wobbled. "We *all* know you're smart, okay? But that doesn't give you the right to *judge* people all the time."

"*Me?*" My mouth dropped open. "I'm not judging you, Ava! I swear I'm not!"

A tear slipped down her cheek. She wiped it away. "You said I 'look bad,' Tally. That's not a judgment?"

"I didn't mean it that way," I said quickly. "I'm sorry if I hurt your feelings. It's just that I'm getting worried—"

"Well, *don't*. Worry about yourself, and why everyone thinks you're such a freak." She grabbed a gym bag and fled the room.

Bleep, I thought. *Why did I say all that? I didn't accomplish anything. In fact, I just made everything between us even worse.* And while I was on the subject of Stupid Negative Comments I'd Made Lately, I took out my phone to see if Spider had texted. No, but why would he? I owed him a major apology, but that should happen in person. After he got back from this boring baseball game he couldn't possibly care about, whatever he'd pretended with Marco.

Then I wondered: Did I owe Sonnet an apology too? I couldn't think what for, but I was starting to wonder if I was capable of talking without causing weirdness. What was wrong with me, anyway? It was like since we got to DC, or maybe to this crazy hotel, I couldn't stop wrecking everything with everybody. Maybe this place was like some alternate dimension where you couldn't shut up and made people hate you. Some kind of eighteenth-century black hole, where you messed up with everyone you cared about, and came out the other end totally friendless. With nothing but an ugly green T-shirt and some stupid pirate Band-Aids that didn't even stick.

Spiffy

A MINUTE LATER THERE WAS a soft knock at the door.

"Hello?" I called.

"Tally, it's me, Ms. Jordan. Can I see you, please?"

"Sure," I said, jumping up to open the door.

She was wearing faded gray sweatpants and a baggy SPCA tee. Non-teacher clothes. This was how she looked when she wasn't at work, and wasn't all scrubbed and perfect and shiny.

I could feel my face relax into a smile. "You look nice," I said.

"Well, thank you, Tally." I could tell she was surprised I'd said a compliment. Who knew, maybe the teachers also thought I was judgy and insulting. I wondered what they thought about Ava.

Ms. Jordan was looking me over. "Mr. G said you weren't feeling well?" she asked kindly.

"I'm okay. Just, you know." I stared at her flip-flops.

"That time of the month?"

"Yeah, I guess," I answered vaguely. "I really just feel like resting tonight."

"A bunch of kids are watching a movie in the Martha Washington conference room. *Monty Python and the Holy Grail.* Have you seen it?"

I shook my head.

"Well, it's hilarious, and knowing you, I think you'd love it."

Knowing me? What a funny thing for her to say. "Maybe later," I said. "Right now, I just feel like resting."

"Okay." She made teacher eye contact. "And I guess I don't have to tell you, do I, that you should stay in your room and not open the door for anyone but Ava or Mrs. Seeley."

"Right-o." I saluted her.

She didn't smile. "Tally, you're *sure* you don't want to see the movie? Because I'd really love for you to join us."

The funny thing was that I believed her. I could tell Ms. Jordan was trying her best to make me part of the group— not to make things easier for *her*, but because she actually wanted to rescue *me*, for some reason. Also, I was starting to think she didn't hate me.

But I still didn't change my mind about going. "Thanks, but no, I'd rather stay here. I promise I'll be fine."

She hesitated. For a second the thought flickered in my mind that I should tell her about Ava. But what would I say, exactly? Ava hadn't admitted anything to me; I had no specific data to report. And if I did tell Ms. Jordan about the eating, or rather the *not* eating, this wouldn't be the right time, anyway. Not when a bunch of kids were waiting for her to show a movie.

Ms. Jordan was studying my face. "Hey, I really like those glasses, Tally. They're spiffy."

I grinned. That was exactly what they were: *spiffy*. I took them off. "Thank you. They belonged to my grandma Wendy, but they're not prescription."

"Well, your grandma Wendy must be very cool."

"She died. But yeah, she really was. She said I took after her, so." I shrugged.

"You know, that's always a compliment, when people say you take after them."

"I guess." Then I said a crazy thing. "Would you like to borrow them tonight?"

"No thanks," Ms. Jordan said. But she grinned back at me. "Although I'd be honored to wear them some other time. Can I please have a rain check?"

"Sure," I answered, although I wondered what rain had to do with wearing spiffy glasses.

Kapow!

THE THING WAS, I REALLY did mean to wash my hair that night. I'm not a big hair-washing sort of person, but once a week or so I get hyperaware of hair grease. And when that happens, I can't keep my hands out of my hair, constantly checking to see if the grease on my scalp has migrated to my hair strands, and everyone I pass on the street is grossing out.

It's the way I always feel when I watch a movie in which the hero (never the heroine) has dirty hair. Usually it's like a Western or something, and not my favorite movie type to begin with, but when the hero has greasy hair, I can't concentrate on anything else. I just sit there the whole time going, *Bleh, why doesn't that guy just wash his hair? And why doesn't anybody* tell *him how gross it looks?*

Anyway. So, yes, I was having a greasy hair day, and after everything that had happened, the idea of a long, soapy shower seemed wonderful. But the problem was, I hadn't packed any shampoo. I could have stolen some of Ava's—and of course she'd consider it "stealing," not "borrowing"—but hers was for Dry and Brittle hair, and my hair wasn't either of those things. For a second I considered using regular soap, but the hotel soap was that George Washington kind, and I didn't trust it. I mean, George Washington wore a powdered wig; who even *knew* what his hair looked like under that thing?

I considered my options. Yes, I'd promised Ms. Jordan I'd stay in my room, but she liked my glasses; this had to mean she was cooler than I'd realized. Even if she wasn't cool, she was a female, which meant she probably understood the greasy-hair issue. And it would be the simplest thing in the world to pop downstairs for a second and buy a small travel-sized bottle of normal, unweird shampoo in Ye Olde Hotel Shoppe, whatever that place was called where I'd bought those excellent pirate Band-Aids.

Before I could chicken out, I took the elevator downstairs to the lobby.

The shoppe was still open, luckily. I found the hair-care shelf right away and grabbed a two-ounce bottle of my favorite shampoo.

Then something caught my eye: KAPOW! it said on the box in red action-comic writing. I took a closer look—it was a bottle of hair color in Sour Apple Green. EXPRESS YOURSELF IN VIVID COLOR! the box shouted. DON'T JUST CHANGE YOUR STYLE—KAPOW!

Obviously, I had to have this.

I grabbed the box and brought it to Mikel, who was once again behind the cash register.

"Hey," he said, grinning at me. "Sardines, right?"

"Excuse me?"

"Yeah, although I looked that up. Sardines don't actually come from Greenland. You were pulling my leg."

My face burned. "I never pull legs."

"Well, you pulled mine, and I fell for it, so woo-hoo for you. You buying that hair color for yourself?"

"For me? No. Are you crazy?"

"Well, it won't work without bleach. You know that, right?"

"Of course. You sell bleach here?"

"Right next to the color. But I'm not sure you should be using it."

"Why not?"

"Because you need a note from your mommy. Back in Greenland." He started sniggering.

I decided to hate him. Without any more chatting, I got the bleach and paid for both boxes.

"Show me how it comes out," Mikel said, still laughing.

Yeah, definitely, you eighteenth-century, mustard-stained mosquito, I thought.

Back upstairs in the room, I put on the Ugly Tee and ripped open the box of hair color. I guess I expected a long, detailed set of instructions inside the box, so I was relieved not to see any. The only instructions were on the bottle: SHAMPOO AND RINSE. WHILE HAIR IS STILL DAMP, APPLY KAPOW! HAIR COLOR. USE GLOVES. LEAVE ON 5-20 MINUTES, DEPENDING ON COLOR PREFERENCE. RINSE, DRY, AND GO!

Well, that seemed easy enough. And quick as popcorn! They even gave you latex gloves in a little plastic bag, which was very considerate of them.

But what about this extra bleach thing? It was funny that the hair-color bottle didn't even mention it. I ripped open the bleach box. Inside was a packet of "lightening bleach" (didn't *all* bleach lighten?), a plastic bottle of KAPOW! Oxide, whatever that was, and a packet of Deep Conditioning Rescue (ditto). Plus, folded into eighths, was a long, complicated list of instructions, in microscopic print. Oh, bleep.

READ FIRST, the instructions yelled at me.

FINE! I yelled back.

1. *Apply ONLY to dry hair.*

What? Already I was lost. The color bottle said to shampoo first. So which was it?

2. *Processing time may vary. Check hair every 10 minutes. Dark brown hair: Process 50-60 minutes. A second application of bleach may be required.*

Curses. An hour of bleaching, and then you *might* have to do another hour? How would you even know? This was worse than bread baking.

3. *Wash hair.*

4. *Apply color to dry hair*

But that wasn't what it said on the bottle of hair color! That bottle said *damp* hair! And what about that Deep Conditioning Rescue stuff? Was I supposed to use it? And if so, when?

Oh, never mind, I told myself. *I'll just figure it out as I go along.*

Sour Apple

THE BLEACHING TOOK FOREVER, but that wasn't the worst thing about it. The worst thing was how it made my scalp feel: all hot and tingly, like there was an army of fire ants zooming around my scalp.

As soon as I felt this, which was right away, I started rubbing my hair. But that didn't stop the ant-army march; it just spread the horrible crawly feeling to my ears and my neck.

And then my shoulders and my back, because now the bleach was dripping down my tee.

Okay, this was unbearable.

I yanked off the Ugly Tee, which maybe I'd be forced to wear again and which was already ugly enough without KAPOW! drips.

But I didn't want bleach dripping directly on my skin, so I needed to wear *something*. But what? Also, the bleach smelled sour, but not like pickle sour. More like if-a-wet-dog-ate-pepperoni-pizza-and-then-barfed sour. So I didn't want that smell on my clothes, because you could tell it would last forever.

Then I remembered that stretchy pink tank Ava had thrown away. She didn't want it, obviously, so who cared if it got a little stinky? And splattery?

I fished it out of the trash, pulled it over my head, and tugged it into place. It didn't completely cover my belly, but close enough. Also, there was something hilarious about wearing Ava's doll-sized pink clothing while dying my hair Sour Apple Green. Too bad I couldn't share the joke of it with anyone.

Then, to take my mind off the fire-ant-scalp feeling, I turned on the TV. They were showing that insipid *Manicure* movie again, and the only thing else remotely watchable was the stupid baseball game. (At first I was confused, because I knew the local team was insect-themed; it took me five minutes to realize they were the *Nats*, not the *Gnats*.) Every time the cameras showed the crowd, I searched for Spider, but I never saw him. Then I remembered Mr. G had gotten way-in-the-back seats, since they were last-minute. Probably the seats were too high up to even see the field. Not that Spider would care, because no way was he interested in the actual game, despite what he said to Marco.

Finally I got so bored I turned off the TV.

But what else was there to do, waiting around while the bleach did its work? All there was to read were a *Welcome to Our Nation's Capital* guidebook, the menu for room service, and a bunch of those fashion magazines Ava wanted to write for someday.

There they were on her night table, in a neat stack, all the corners touching. I flipped through a few of them: *She. OnTrend. CelebStyle. ModeJunior.* Nothing but pages of pretzel-stick, clonewoman models looking grumpy, probably because they were hungry for muffins.

TEN FASHION "IT" GIRLS

LOOKS YOU GOTTA HAVE FOR FALL

STAR WATCH: AWARD SEASON FASHION!

WHO ROCKED WHAT

Yawn. I mean, sure, there were also articles, but I totally didn't get what Ava saw in them. Although there had to be *something*, because Ava wasn't stupid. And it definitely surprised me how she said she wanted to write this stuff, because I never saw her writing just for fun. Not that I would, of course. Because writing was private.

But then I thought of something: *Ava writes in her yellow notebook!* Before I could stop myself, I lifted her pillow. There it was.

I was crazy with boredom, the room was empty, my scalp was on fire, and I had to kill time *some*how—so I had a peek. Today there were only two numbers: 110 and 75. Which was odd, I thought, because I distinctly remembered her doing one hundred sit-ups this morning. Why had she written 110?

Unless the number counted something else.

Like what?

Maybe I hadn't solved the mystery, after all.

The doorknob was turning, so I slipped Ava's notebook under her pillow.

"Tally, what are you doing?" Ava was standing in the room, pale and dripping with sweat.

"Nothing," I said. "I needed something to read while my processing was . . . *processing*, so—"

"You went searching on my night table? For a magazine?" She kicked off her sneakers. Considering how she'd acted during our last conversation, she seemed way calmer now, I thought. Maybe she'd burned off something in the gym. "Is that my tank you're wearing?"

"Yeah," I said, blushing. Which only made my scalp feel hotter. "You threw it away, so I thought, you know, while my hair was dripping all over the place—"

"Whatever. It doesn't fit you, Tally, but you can have it. I hate how it looks on me. And not that it's my business, but what are you doing to your hair?"

I tried to sound confident. "Expressing myself with color."

"Expressing *what*, exactly?"

"Well, it's called Sour Apple."

"Oh. Why am I not surprised." Ava sniffed the air. "It doesn't *smell* like sour apple."

"It's the bleach. First you put it on and wait. *Then* you add the color."

"How long have you had it on?"

"The bleach? Like thirty minutes."

"*Like* thirty minutes? Or thirty minutes?"

"Ava, I was watching TV. I don't know *precisely*."

"Well, if you color your hair, you *need* to know precisely! You're supposed to use a timer!"

"That's not what it said in the instructions."

"Yeah? Let me see." She held out her hand impatiently, so I gave her the instructions.

She squinted at the tiny print. "So have you been checking the color every ten minutes, like it says?"

"No. Well, I mean, not exactly."

"Tally, what's *wrong* with you? If you don't do it *exactly* how they say, it'll come out terrible!"

"Ava, I think you're overreacting."

"No, Tally, I think you're *under*reacting!"

Ava was starting to make me nervous. It was impossible to deny that I'd been careless about the directions, and Ava seemed so sure of herself. Besides, she was Miss Perfection; I was used to her getting As for neatness, following directions, filling in all the blanks.

And by then I couldn't ignore the fact that I was sweating. Not regular sweat, like when you jog uphill. I mean, panic sweat.

"I think I'm done, though," I announced.

"Already?" Ava said. "Are you sure it's been at least fifty minutes?"

"No. But I'm pretty sure it's enough."

Before she could correct me again, I raced into the shower, still wearing the tank top. But the hotel had one of those complicated knobs (twist clockwise for temperature, counterclockwise for water pressure) so at first I sprayed my head with jets of scalding hot water.

Which was not the effect I was going for.

I yelped.

"You okay?" Ava shouted from outside the bathroom.

"Yep. Just a bit tingly."

I finally adjusted the water to a cool spray, and my scalp stopped screaming at me. Although it still felt angry as I towel-dried my hair over the sink.

When it was dryish, I checked the mirror. My hair did look lighter in places—but it was wet, so I couldn't be sure of the total effect. And I was supposed to add the color when my hair was still damp, wasn't I? At least, that's what it said on the hair-color bottle.

I poured the entire bottle of color over my head. Now I had this awful-smelling liquid oozing down my neck and back, trickling down my cheeks. I didn't want to use the white hotel towels to mop it off, because what if they turned Sour Apple Green and my parents had to pay extra to replace them? So I stepped back into the shower for a second, just to rinse the extra ooze off my body.

And there was nothing else to do but wait. I sat on the edge of the tub, checking my phone to see if Spider had texted me. But he hadn't. So I watched puppies on YouTube for a bit. Then a baby hedgehog.

"What's going on now?" Ava asked through the closed bathroom door.

"Nothing. I put on the color a few minutes ago."

"With what?"

"What do you mean?"

"You didn't use my brush, did you?"

Bleep. The instructions said "Brush in," not "Pour on"! "Of course I didn't! I wouldn't just use your *stuff*, Ava. So anyway, now it's just waiting."

"For how long?"

"Well, that's up to me. But I want it extremely bright green."

"No comment. You're checking the time, I hope?"

"Of course I am!"

"You have something to read in there?"

"Not really."

The door opened, and in walked Ava with the fashion magazines.

"That's okay," I said immediately, holding up my hand like I was stopping traffic. "I don't actually read stuff like that."

"Why not?" Ava sat on the edge of the tub. "Don't be such a snob, Tally."

"I'm not! I know you like them, but truthfully I don't get it. A bunch of boring girls wearing boring outfits—"

"*I* think the outfits are beautiful. And how do you know those girls are boring? They could be musicians or incredible athletes—"

"If they were athletes, they wouldn't be so skinny. Those girls are starving—or else somebody made them look that way, which is even sicker. In real life they probably all have zits and overbites. And *actual bellies*—"

Ava groaned. "Oh, Tally. Do you *ever* shut up? And for your information, the articles are brilliant." She flipped open *ModeJunior* to an article called "Ten Paths to POWER (When You're Too Young To Vote)."

"All right," I said. "That looks sort of interesting, I guess."

"There's also this cool feature every month called WILAM—What I Like About Me—and readers write in weird stuff about themselves, like the fact that their eyes are crossed or they have outie belly buttons."

"Okay, *that's* cool. But the models are still super creepy. They look like starving aliens."

"*Fine.*" Ava stomped out of the bathroom. "*Don't* read my magazines. I was just trying to be nice."

"Thanks, though," I called after her, but she didn't answer.

I sat there for a few more minutes, seeing tessellations in the floor tiles. Finally I couldn't stand the sticky, oozy-neck feeling any longer, so I stuck my head into the sink and rinsed the dye out.

"Behold," I announced, as I stepped out of the bathroom.

Rescue

"ARE YOU *SURE* THAT'S SOUR APPLE?" Ava asked. Her eyes were huge.

"Definitely. Why, it doesn't look appley to you?"

"Not . . . incredibly. But your hair is still pretty wet, right? It needs to be dry to get the whole effect. You should borrow my blow-dryer. And I have some other hair products you should probably use too."

I thought about all of Ava's bottles on the edge of the sink. No way was I going to spend even *more* time on this endless hair stuff, which was worse than baking bread, worse than a seven-layer cake. "Thanks," I said firmly. "But I'm done. I'll just blow-dry it now. As is."

"Are you sure?" Ava said. "Because it'll come out fried without conditioner."

"I'm totally, completely positive."

She shrugged. "Whatever. It's your hair, Tally."

That was when I remembered the Rescue stuff. But probably it was too late to be Rescued, I told myself—and anyway, I wasn't showing Ava I had any doubts. I plugged in her hair dryer by the sink and waved it first at my damp torso, then at my head. Again, my scalp was feeling hot and prickly as the hot air blew my hair dry.

But at least now results were visible. Although under the bathroom lights, the color was confusing. Orangey at the roots, tree-bark mossy on the bottom. Not the Granny Smith green I'd been imagining. Not remotely.

Also, my hair felt like straw. Old straw that fat horses stepped on.

Ava came into the bathroom. "Tally, what—omigod. Your *hair*."

"I know!"

"Does it say anything in the instructions? I mean about what to do." She held the bottle up to her eyes. Then she scanned the bottle of bleach. But there was nothing she read there that she wanted to read out loud. "Tally, where did you get this stuff, anyway?"

"Downstairs in the lobby. I just bought it like an hour ago. Well, more like two hours."

"You went to that little hotel shop? It looks so gross in there."

"I know, I know! But that's kind of irrelevant at this moment, don't you think?"

Because *the color*. Oh, bleepity bleep! Now that my hair was dry, you could tell that the color—if you could call it a color—was a disaster. I looked like a tree monster, an Ent. Or no: like the Swamp Thing.

"Try to stay calm," Ava urged, watching me stare at myself in the mirror.

I almost laughed. "Are you serious? How can I stay calm about *this*?"

"Because you're Tally. You don't *care* what people think, right?"

I snorted. "I thought you said I *did* care. Deep down. But that I was only pretending I didn't!"

"Yeah, well. I think you care about *some* things. Just not about how you look."

"Ava, that's totally wrong, okay? *Of course* I care! I just don't want someone telling me what I *should* look like. Not some stupid fashion magazine, or the internet. Or my mom."

Her face flushed. "Are you saying that's how *I* am?"

"Well, yeah. I mean, aren't you?"

Three sharp knocks on the door.

Ava and I stared at each other in horror. We both knew who knocked like that.

"Ava, sweetie, can I come in?" Mrs. Seeley called in a cheery voice. "I just want to say good night."

"Just a minute, Mom." She threw a towel at me. "Put it on your head!" she hissed.

"Put a towel on my *head*?"

"Pretend you just washed your hair! And cover up my tank!"

I grabbed another towel and wrapped it around my torso.

As soon as Ava opened the door, Mrs. Seeley's nostrils flared. "What's that smell?"

"I don't smell anything," Ava said, sniffing.

"You don't? It's like rotten meat."

"Oh, it's just my shampoo," I said, as if the answer just came to me. "My dad hates it. He says it stinks up the bathroom whenever I use it."

"I'm sure he does." Mrs. Seeley scrunched her nose just like Ava. "Anyway, I just got a text from Mr. G. He said they had a great time at the game, and they're on their way back to the hotel. Ava, honey, you ate your dinner?"

"Not yet. I wanted to shower first after the gym, and Tally was washing her hair, so—"

"That's true," I said eagerly. "I was!"

Mrs. Seeley waved her hand in front of her nose. "Tally, dear, whatever's in that shampoo can't be good for your hair. It smells really *vile*."

"I agree! It's the last time I ever use it, I promise."

"Good. Why don't you turn up the air-conditioning, to get more circulation in here." She walked over to the thermostat and pressed a button. Immediately we could hear a fan whoosh on from somewhere in the walls.

Oxygen, yay!

Mrs. Seeley kissed Ava's cheek. "Well, good night, you two. See you at breakfast."

"Thanks," I told Ava as she shut the door behind her mother.

"What for," Ava said, shrugging.

I couldn't explain. But somehow, right then, it felt as if we were on the same team. Us versus Mrs. Seeley. It was a strange sensation, and I wondered if Ava thought so too.

I took off the towels and hung them in the bathroom. Ava walked over to her plastic container of dinner. She took out a few red grapes, popped them into her mouth, and dumped the rest into the trash.

"You aren't hungry?" I asked.

"Nope. And I refuse to be nagged, Tally."

"Sorry. I won't nag you, then."

"Thanks." She reached for her notebook and wrote something fast.

"So what's in the notebook, anyway?" I said.

"None of your business," she replied, not looking at me. And I think it was that sentence—*None of your business*—that gave me the answer.

I stared at her. "It's about food, isn't it," I said. "What are the numbers you keep writing—like calories or something?"

She shut the notebook. "Wait. Tally, you *read* it?"

"I just looked at it. When you left it out."

Ava's face crumpled. And then this happened so fast it was a blur: She grabbed her phone and snapped a photo. Of me.

"Ava, what—" I began.

She held up her phone so I could see the picture: Me with slime-green, strawlike hair sticking out wildly.

Me wearing Ava's incredibly clingy pink tank, all blotchy and discolored from the bleach. My bare belly sticking out at the bottom. My eyes in shock.

"Tally," Ava was saying through her teeth, "if you tell my mom, or Nadia, or anyone else, about my notebook, or about throwing out food, or about the muffin, or lunch, or anything *else* that's none of your business, I'll post this photo *online*."

"Are you serious?"

"And I'll show it to your boyfriend!"

"You mean Spider? He won't care."

She laughed. It wasn't a nice laugh, either. "No, not *Spider*. I mean the boy you secretly like, *Marco*."

"Fine, Ava! Go ahead! I really don't—"

"I'll make sure other people see too." Her eyes flashed. "I'll show it to Sonnet! And then you'll find out if she's still your friend."

For a second I couldn't speak. Then I could. "Ava, that's horrible! *You're* horrible! I was stupid to worry about you!"

"Hey, so we finally agree about something," Ava replied.

The Cap

AFTER THAT I CONSIDERED TEXTING Fiona about the hair disaster, and also about Ava's behavior. But I decided against it: My sister would probably ask for a photo, and I couldn't bear to take a selfie. Plus, I was pretty sure she'd tell Mom—and even though I was dreading that conversation, I knew I should have it myself, when we got home. There was no point typing up the whole story now, and then having to talk about it all over again as soon as I got off the bus. Once would be bad enough.

So I just crawled into bed. But as I lay there on the

battle-pattern sheets, all I could think about was how much I missed my dog, Spike. At home her blanket-hogging kept me awake sometimes, but that night I didn't even care about sleeping. I just needed the warm weight of her doggy body. Even her snoring and her stinky breath would have been a comfort. And thinking about her soothing wonderfulness made me vow that when I got home, I'd take her for an extra-long walk in the park. Then I'd get her a double-scoop vanilla ice cream cone—a special treat she usually got on her adoptaversary.

Somehow, picturing Spike's calm brown eyes, I fell asleep.

And when I awoke, Ava wasn't there. This was really good news. Because after everything that had happened between us, I didn't know how to share a room with her anymore, be all, "Ho-hum, whatever, dibs on the first shower." Now all I could think was: *How could I possibly have believed, even for one millisecond, that Ava Seeley and I were on the same team? She'll never be on my team; she'll only humiliate me and judge me. I was such a moron to care about her eating habits. Or non-eating habits.*

Anyway, not having to deal with her that morning was a huge relief.

The other good news was that I remembered that I'd

brought my purple newsboy cap. So if I kept my cap on all day—glued it to my scalp for the entire rest of the trip—probably no one would see my Ent-head. And the thing about dressing funny all the time: If one day you're dressing funny *for a reason*, people probably won't suspect anything. They'll just go, *Oh, look, there's Tally being Tally.*

But just in case anyone got too focused on my cap, I added my ringtail-lemur necklace. As a decoy, sort of. Then I went downstairs for breakfast.

Where, shockingly, Spider was sitting at a table by himself, eating a toasted bagel.

"Hey," I greeted him, holding a bowl of granola and a glass of OJ. And trying to look normal, like I hadn't been the worst friend in the world to him just twelve hours ago. "How was the game last night?"

"Boring," he said.

So I sat down with him. Because yay, Spider was still Spider. And yay, he was telling the truth again. And wasn't too mad to talk to me.

"But I had fun, anyway," he said. "Also I'm sorry I yelled at you like that."

"No, *I* need to be the one apologizing." I took a giant chilly sip of OJ. "Spider, I'm really just *incredibly* sorry about what I said to you yesterday. I think it's great that you've made friends with Marco, and of course I get that he's changed. And you, too," I added. *"Really."*

Spider smiled. "Thanks, Tally. But I knew you were feeling sick when you said all those things, so." Before I could confess the truth about *that*, he said, "Hey, I found out who Marco was talking to on the phone: his little brother."

"Oh. I didn't know he had one."

"Yeah, well. He doesn't show up much at stuff. He's six years old and he's autistic and doesn't talk. And he has meltdowns—not like what I used to have, way worse. Marco says he's the only one in his family who can calm him down, so it's a big deal that he's away from home on this trip."

"Okay," I said, but only because I didn't know what else to say. Back when Marco's dad was Spider's Little League coach, I always thought he was a mean, impatient man—so it didn't surprise me that he couldn't deal with a little kid's meltdown. But hearing that Marco could, and that he did it all the time . . . something happened to me. Inside me, I mean.

I looked across the restaurant, where Marco was sitting with Trey, Jamal, and some other boys. Really, he had a very nice smile, I thought. Sweet, and not the slightest bit smirky like Trey's.

Suddenly his eyes caught mine, and he smiled at me. At *me*.

I felt my cheeks flush and my scalp tingle inside the cap.

I sipped some more OJ.

Just then Ava and her mom walked into the restaurant. As soon as Mrs. Seeley spotted me, she waved and headed over.

Oh, bleepity bleep. I tugged the cap to cover my ears.

"So how's it going with Ava?" Spider murmured.

"Long story," I murmured back.

"Good morning!" Mrs. Seeley exclaimed. "Are these seats taken? Are you all set for a *supreme morning*?"

Spider and I looked at each other. I hadn't even glanced at today's schedule.

"I'm not sure. What's happening today?" I asked casually.

"You don't know? This morning we're sitting in on a session of the United States Supreme Court!" Mrs. Seeley spooned some oatmeal into her mouth; the spoon clinked against her teeth. "And afterward we're going to the US Botanic Garden, where they have the most *perfect* roses, and also a museum or two. Tally, dear, you really should have a look at the schedule! Ava, darling, aren't you getting tired of vanilla yogurt?"

Ava stirred her container. "No," she said flatly. "Because

it's what I *want*, Mom." She turned to me. "Hey, Tally, I like your hat."

Why did she just say that? I couldn't help thinking she was repeating her threat—warning me that if I said anything to her mom, she'd blab about the hair fiasco. Or worse than blab: share the hideous photo. I mean, it would be bad enough if people saw my horror-movie hair. But what would really be unbearable: *They'd see me in Ava's teeny pink tank top.* Looking like a clonegirl wannabe. Looking all wrong for my "body type." All wrong for me.

"Thank you," I answered Ava, avoiding Spider's eyes.

Rules Are Rules

AT SEVEN THIRTY WE WERE all in the hotel lobby. Sonnet waved at me, but she was sticking close to Haley, so I just waved back.

"All right, folks, listen up," Mr. G said. "Today's our last full day, and it's going to be exciting. This morning, we're off to the US Supreme Court to sit in on an actual oral argument."

"I'd rather see the National Zoo than the court thing," Trey said. "They have giant pandas there, right?"

Immediately Nadia, Haley, and Sonnet started going, "Ooooh, pandas, they're sooo cuuute."

Mr. G, though, was not going to be swayed. I guess the time for student input was over. "We're doing the Supreme Court, people," he said firmly. "It will be an experience."

"Everything is an *experience*," Trey muttered. "That doesn't mean it's *fun*."

Other kids were agreeing with Trey, but not me. After missing out on the Kennedy Center tour, I wanted to see *something* special on this trip—and watching the Supreme Court in action, deciding a case that affected millions of people, would definitely qualify.

Mr. G said we'd be taking the DC Metro to Union Station, and that we needed to leave almost immediately—visitor seating was first come, first served, which meant you needed to line up early. Oral arguments started at ten on the dot, and first we'd have to get through security. Which was especially strict, he said: no backpacks, bags, or even cell phones were allowed in the courtroom. There were lockers at the court, but he didn't want to waste time dealing with them—so we should plan to leave all those items here, at the hotel.

"Let's leave Spider," Trey said.

Marco punched his arm and told him to shut up.

Then a funny thing happened: Marco looked over at me. And because I'd been looking at *him*, our eyes met for a second. Just long enough for my heart to start skittering.

And also just long enough for Ava to notice and smile at me in a teasing sort of way. Like: *See? Told you he was your boyfriend.*

We returned to our rooms to dump our phones and bags and stuff, met back in the lobby, and then hopped on the Metro for a few stops. By the time we got to the Court at eight fifteen, a line of people snaked in the plaza in front of the building.

"Will we even get *in*?" Nadia grumbled. "Mr. G, I don't want to wait out here for nothing."

"They begin seating at nine thirty," Mr. G said. He wasn't smiling or anything; I could tell he was really serious about this. Maybe, I thought, it was *his* obsession.

The whole time we were out on that plaza, the wind was swirling like it does when it's testing itself to see if it's really autumn. The cap fit snugly on my head, but every time one of those wind gusts happened, I panicked a little, holding it on my head with both hands, just in case. So far that morning, no one had commented on it, not even Sonnet, who always noticed my outfits. But of course she was hanging mostly with Haley and Nadia, all of them wearing skirts that rippled in the wind—and Ava, who, in her black top and black skinny jeans, looked like a mini-version of one of those pencil-shaped fashion mag clonemodels.

At exactly nine thirty, we were waved into the "three-minute line." Stern-looking police officers began walking back and forth, eying us, announcing all the things that weren't allowed inside the Court, and where you could store stuff in lockers and checkrooms.

A poke to my shoulder.

"Young lady," a policewoman said. "No hats, please."

"Excuse me?" I said.

"No hats permitted inside. You can store it in a locker. Or else the checkroom, which is located—"

"No, that's impossible." I felt my scalp tingling. "I *can't* store my hat."

She frowned at me. "Why not?"

"It's . . . personal."

Everyone was staring now. I mean, not just Eastview Middle School kids, including Spider and Marco. The whole line.

"You want to step over here, young lady?" the policewoman asked in a loud, impatient voice. She wasn't actually *asking*, I realized.

Ms. Jordan put her hand on my shoulder. "Come on, Tally," she murmured. "Don't worry, I'm coming with you."

My brain was numb, so I let her lead me to the police-woman, whose badge said OFFICER BUMBRY.

"Officer, good morning," Ms. Jordan said pleasantly. "This girl is my seventh grade history student. Today is our last day in town on a school field trip, and she didn't mean—"

"Rules are rules," Officer Bumbry cut in. She looked at me with hard eyes. "You think rules don't apply to you, young lady?"

I shook my head, hoping that Ava wasn't listening, but knowing she was, along with everyone else.

"Good," Officer Bumbry said. "Then I need to ask you again to remove the hat. Now, please."

"But I *can't*," I wailed, and burst into tears. Not a few sniffles, either—loud snotty ugly-crying. Kind of a melt-down, I guess you could call it.

I can't even say what happened next—only that I was being led away from the plaza by Ava and Mrs. Seeley.

"Tally, it's fine," Ava was saying. "Who needs to see that stuff, anyway."

"Me!" I blubbered. "I didn't get to go to the Kennedy Center, this whole trip has been a disaster, and I really *wanted* to go inside!"

"Talia, dear, the United States Supreme Court's not going anywhere," Mrs. Seeley said, reaching into her pocket for a neatly folded tissue, which she handed to me. "Any time you want, you can come back here and just get in line. It's always open to the public when the Court is in session."

"I guess," I said, blowing my nose. But I knew it wouldn't happen for a long, long time. When your parents run a bakery, they need to be there every day. No big family vacations in *my* future.

The three of us walked against the wind, not talking. Finally Mrs. Seeley asked, almost gently, "So, Tally dear, can you explain the problem with your hat?"

I glanced at Ava. Truthfully, I was shocked she hadn't already told her mom about my hair disaster. But of course there was plenty of stuff she wasn't sharing with her mom these days.

Ava nodded at me like: *Go ahead, Tally. You might as well. You have no choice, anyway.*

I took a deep, shaky breath. By then we were back at the train station, so although plenty of people were rushing by us on their way to work, I decided it was okay to take the cap off. None of these people knew me. None of them would judge me, and even if they did, I'd never see them again, so it didn't matter.

I took off my cap.

"Oh, poor baby," Mrs. Seeley cried, nearly smothering me in a hug.

Roomies

WE NEVER GOT ON THE train. Instead the three of us walked around town for a couple of hours. I explained the KAPOW! ordeal, and Mrs. Seeley told some funny stories about her own hair disasters when she was younger, like how when she was in college, she used a curling iron once and it short-circuited or something, frying off an entire section of hair. So then her roommate, Sarah—the one who worked at the Kennedy Center now—had the idea to give them both crazy haircuts as camouflage, and to tell everyone they were starting a "neo-punk girl band."

That image—Mrs. Seeley with shaved-off punk hair, in a pretend girl band—was so ridiculous it gave me the giggles. Ava, too.

Mrs. Seeley put her arms around us both. "Roomies are so important," she said. "A good roommate is even more important than a friend."

My eyes met Ava's for just a second before she turned away.

Then Mrs. Seeley told me about her "hair person" back in Eastview. "Patrick is a genius," she said. "I'm sure he can do something to fix that color."

"What about the way my hair *feels*?" I held up a handful of straw.

"He'll make it better," Mrs. Seeley replied firmly. "And remember, *hair is just hair*; it always grows back! Nothing you do to it is ever permanent, not even a permanent." She smiled at her lame joke. "But next time, Tally, dear, swear you won't use inferior products you know nothing about."

"And follow the directions," Ava added, rolling her eyes. "And use conditioner."

I promised, even though I couldn't imagine doing anything with hair for the rest of my life.

After a while, we figured that the Eastviewers had

finished with the Supreme Court and were onto the next activity. And we could have joined them if we wanted. But Ava said she wasn't eager to hang out with Nadia, and did we *really* have to do a bunch of museums on such a pretty day?

Suddenly I remembered how Mrs. Seeley had said she wanted to see the "perfect roses."

"I guess we could do the Botanic Garden?" I told her. "I feel really bad you won't get to go."

"Oh, Tally, don't be silly," Mrs. Seeley scoffed. "Roses are just roses! I can see them anywhere, anytime. I'd rather spend today seeing things we can't see anywhere else."

That was how we ended up at the National Zoo. It was a very fun afternoon, actually. We saw the pandas and the great cats and the Asian elephants—but I have to say, I liked the small-mammals exhibit the best. The meerkats were hilarious, the way they sat up on their hind legs and made rude eye contact, and I couldn't stop giggling at one species with the name Screaming Hairy Armadillo. The next time Trey bothered me, I vowed, that's what I'd call him: *You Screaming Hairy Armadillo.* That was, if I could say it without giggling.

As for Ava, the whole time, she was smiley and friendly.

Of course, her mom was there, so she couldn't have been outright nasty—but she also didn't have to laugh at my jokes, or keep asking where I wanted to go next, or if I was hungry for lunch. To be honest, I kept thinking she was being a little *too* nice, and it made me uncomfortable. Because why *should* she be nice? She'd made it clear that she didn't like me.

Plus, *if* for some crazy reason she *had* changed her mind about me, the first thing she'd have done was delete the photo. The second thing would have been to prove it, showing me how it was gone from her phone, never to be seen by anyone, ever. But she didn't do either—so the entire afternoon as we strolled the zoo, I knew she could still turn on me again without warning. All I had to do was mention her eating issues to anyone—out of worry about her, not spite—and the photo of me squeezed into Ava's tiny pink top, with Slime Thing hair, would go viral.

So, despite the break from our classmates, and the sunshine, and the Screaming Hairy Armadillos, and everyone's niceness, I couldn't relax. Mrs. Seeley bought us bags of popcorn, but I could barely eat any. It also didn't help when Ava ordered herself a chicken salad sandwich for lunch—and dumped 95 percent of it in the trash as soon as her mom stepped into the ladies' room.

She gave me a sideways look when she did it, like she was daring me to say something. But I didn't; I couldn't. She was keeping the photo a secret from the entire class, I told myself, so I had to keep her secret too.

When we got back to the Hotel Independence, it was late afternoon. As we stepped into the elevator, I thanked Mrs. Seeley and Ava for the ninety-ninth time that day.

"My pleasure, dear," Mrs. Seeley said. "Tell your lovely mom to call Patrick ASAP. In fact, if she calls him now, you can see him tomorrow evening, as soon as we get off the bus."

"Mom, maybe Tally hasn't told her mom about the hair thing yet," Ava said.

"You *haven't*?" Mrs. Seeley asked me, raising her perfect eyebrows, as if she couldn't imagine a daughter not sharing everything.

"I wanted to do it in person," I explained.

"Well, give her some warning first, Tally, dear. Moms shock easily."

Did mine? I couldn't say; I'd never shocked her before.

When the elevator arrived on Lexington, Mrs. Seeley told us she'd be taking a nap and would see us later—but she didn't specify when, and Ava didn't ask. By then I was exhausted and sweaty. All I wanted to do was to take off my wool cap and get into the shower.

Not Ava. "I think I'll head over to the gym," she announced, stretching her arms.

I glanced at Mrs. Seeley, to see if she was surprised Ava needed more exercise after all the walking we'd done. But she didn't react. "Call your dad," she told Ava. "But don't tell him I told you to."

"I was planning to call him on my own," Ava replied. "You don't need to *remind* me, Mom."

Suddenly the hallway felt chilly, like the three of us were standing under a vent of air-conditioning. Mrs. Seeley was frowning at Ava. "Frankly, I just don't want him calling *me* complaining that you never call him."

"I *always* call him, Mom. Just that *one time* I didn't!"

"Well, he made it sound like more than once. Anyway, I don't have the stomach for this, Ava! Just return his calls and leave me out of it, please."

We watched Mrs. Seeley slip her key card into her door.

As soon as Ava and I entered our room, the first thing Ava did was head for the bathroom sink, where she filled a glass and drank. When the glass was empty, she filled another and drank it all. Then she asked me if I planned to take a shower.

"Ugh, definitely," I groaned, flinging my cap across the room and flopping on the bed.

"What I mean is, could you please take it now? I need to make a phone call. In private."

"Oh. Sure." The last thing I felt like doing was arguing, so I got up from the bed and headed into the bathroom.

Right away I turned on the water. But I didn't get into the shower. I didn't say to myself, *Hey, cool, a golden opportunity for eavesdropping*. Although I had to admit I was curious. What was going on between Ava and her dad? What was going on between Ava's parents? Were they splitting up? Had they already split?

And how was Ava dealing? The more time I spent with her, the less I knew. It was like she had googols of stuff locked up inside her, in a silo that reached the moon.

I pressed my ear to the door.

"No, Daddy, I wasn't ignoring you—

"I love you, too. But I don't want to hear that stuff about Mom—

"No, I'm *not* taking sides—

"No, I refuse—

"That isn't fair! You can't just—

"You are? When?

"You always say that but you never—

"Yeah, I will. Okay, I promise. Gotta go now.

"To the gym! Yeah, there's a decent one here.

"I know. I'll be careful. I told you I promised—

"Love you, Daddy. I will. Bye."

I got into the shower fast.

When I came out of the bathroom, Ava was on the floor, not moving.

Cartwheel

"AVA! OMIGOD! ARE YOU OKAY?"

Her eyes opened, and for a second she looked at me as if she thought she might be dreaming. Then, slowly, she sat up and groaned.

"Oh crap, I think I fainted," Ava said.

"You did?"

"Don't shout. God, Tally. Haven't you ever seen anyone faint before?"

"No! Why would I?"

"Because people faint all the time. It's not a big deal."

"Oh yes, it is! Are you serious? It *totally* is! We should call a doctor!"

"No, Tally, we should *not*."

"Okay, I'll tell your mom, then. *She* can decide if—"

"Tally, *no*." Ava grabbed my arm. For someone who'd just fainted, she had a strong grip. "I was just light-headed from walking in the sun all afternoon. And being super dehydrated. Could you please just get me a glass of water?"

I took the glass she'd already emptied and refilled it in the bathroom sink. When I handed it to her, she drank it in almost one gulp.

"Thanks," she said, wiping her mouth with the back of her hand. "Tally, you really need to leave my mom out of this."

"Why?"

She took a few seconds to speak. "I don't really want to talk about it, okay?"

"Ava, you *have* to tell me. If you don't, I'm just getting your mom."

"*No*."

"Then tell me!"

"All right. But this is just between us." She sighed; I could tell she hadn't talked about this before, and she said the words slowly. "So my parents are going through something bad right now. They're not getting along *at all*—they're separated, and I'm scared they're getting divorced. Well, I'm pretty *sure* they are. And I'm basically caught in the middle, you know?"

I nodded, even though I didn't know. My parents loved each other, and they got along great. We all did, really.

"Promise you won't tell anyone," she added. "I haven't told my friends yet. Not even Nadia."

"How come?"

"Because Mom said not to. She doesn't want gossip."

"Well, I wouldn't, anyway," I said. "I can keep a secret! Besides, I never talk to Nadia."

"Well, don't tell Sonnet, then."

Not a problem, I thought. *We're barely talking anymore, anyway.*

"Tally? Can I tell you something?" Ava asked, almost shyly. "Mom's under a lot of stress right now, and I don't want to worry her over nothing. She seems incredibly strong, I know, but this whole thing with my dad . . ." She blew out some air.

Should I just shut up? Yes, but I couldn't. "Ava, your mom is *already* freaked about you," I said. "About the whole eating thing."

Ava blinked. "How do you know that?"

"Because it's obvious! She's always noticing your food. And she's been asking *me* about it."

"She has? And what did you tell her?"

"Whatever you'd want me to say. Nothing, basically."

"Well, thank you." She bit her lip. "Honestly, Tally, I just don't have an appetite lately. And I can't keep anything down if I *do* eat. Mom knows it's all because of the divorce thing, so if you tell her I'm not eating, it'll just make her feel guilty. And then *I'll* feel worse, and I'll eat even *less*. Anyhow, she hasn't been sleeping lately, and right now she's napping, which is great, so *please* don't disturb her, okay, Tally? You owe her; she was so nice to you today, right?"

"Yeah, she was," I admitted.

"You know, she really wanted to see those roses. And she didn't because of *you*."

I winced. "I know!"

"So you should take back what you said about her. How she's so bossy and intense—"

"I never said 'bossy,'" I protested. "And I'm very sorry I said all that other stuff, okay? But I'm still worried."

"About what? I swear I'm *absolutely fine* now. Want to see me do a cartwheel?"

"*Now?* Ava, are you *nuts*?"

"Watch." She jumped up, flung open the door, and did two cartwheels, one after the other, down the hotel hallway. Then she turned around and grinned at me. "So? Are you convinced?"

"I guess," I said slowly. "I mean, okay, that was amazing. But, Ava, I really, really think—"

"Then you're wrong," she called over her shoulder, as she ran down the hall toward the staircase.

The Key

THE WAY MY FRIENDS HAD been telling me not to help them anymore, to stop acting like a babysitter or a rescue dolphin, hurt a lot. I mean, *a lot*. So now a part of me was yelling at myself: *Just mind your own business, Tally.*

But I knew that Ava was in trouble—real trouble—and that I couldn't just do nothing. Except what *could* I do, exactly? Wake Mrs. Seeley? Call an ambulance? Wait for Ms. Jordan to come back to the hotel, and then tell her everything? Even if I did, I wasn't sure what I could say: *Ava fainted before, but she's fine now. Ava just did two cartwheels and ran off to the gym, and I'm worried because she should be tired.*

Plus, just now she'd opened up to me, telling me things even her friends didn't know—so how could I turn around and blab about the fainting? What I didn't think was: *Oh, and if I do tell someone, she'll send around that hideous photo.* At least, I didn't think that I was thinking it. Probably it was in my mind, but way at the back, just kind of bubbling away, like the stew Mom makes in the winter and leaves on the stove all day—but I wasn't aware of it. I was thinking about Ava, about what (if anything) I could do to make sure she was okay.

And the only thing I could think was: *Go check on her in the gym.* If Ava seemed wobbly or weak or pale, I'd definitely tell Mrs. Seeley she'd fainted.

But where was the gym? I had no idea. I could call the front desk from back in the room and ask—but as I stood there in the hallway and reached into my pocket for the key card, I instantly became aware of three things:

1) It wasn't in the pocket

2) Of the hotel robe I was still wearing.

3) Also, there was nothing on my head besides Swamp Monster–colored hair. . . .

BLEEP. I WAS LOCKED OUT OF THE ROOM. And now I'd have to go downstairs in a terry-cloth bathrobe and an exposed slime head to beg for a substitute key. From people wearing bonnets and dancing jigs. *Bleepity bleepity bleep!*

But there was no choice. I raced down the stairs to the lobby.

The front desk was empty. Where was everybody? At a quilting bee? Writing amendments to the Constitution?

"*Helloooo,*" I called out. "*Anyone hoooome?*"

Hipster Bonnet sauntered over to the front desk, not curtseying or anything. "Good afternoon, may I help you?"

I finally got a look at her name tag: CARLY. Didn't match her costume, but whatever. "Yes! I'm locked out of my room, and—"

"Girl, what's the deal with your hair?"

I winced. "It got kapowed."

"It sure did. Holy crap. You should cover that *up.*"

"I agree. But my hat's in the room. Which I'm locked out of. Which is why I'm *here.*"

"Got it. You want to borrow something? We Colonials are big on headgear." She started searching through some shelves behind the desk.

"I really just want another key to my room. Lexington oh-six. *Please*," I added loudly, trying to do Ava's imitation of her mother.

"No problem, just give me one sec." She typed something, drummed her fingers, then handed me a fresh key card. "Although, hold on, I *know* we have some extra—"

Carly disappeared behind the desk. When she popped up again, she was holding a bonnet, a three-cornered hat, and a powdered wig. "Staff leave these around, and sometimes guests want some as souvenirs, so we're always well stocked. In my personal opinion, you want to go with the bonnet, but—"

Just then there was a commotion behind us. I could hear shouts and loud laughing and girls' voices singing "My Shot" from *Hamilton*, and a male grown-up voice yelling, *"Quiet, folks!"* and somebody protesting about someone else pushing.

My classmates returning from their afternoon activities.

I am not throwing away my shot!

I froze.

"Just take any one, okay?" Carly urged. "On the house."

"Thanks," I mumbled.

I grabbed the powdered wig, plopped it on my head, and fled up the stairs.

Lightning

AS SOON AS I STEPPED into my room, I flicked on the lights and checked the bathroom: no sign of Ava. Probably she was still in the hotel gym, doing cartwheels—but maybe she was lying on the floor, with no one around to give her a glass of water. I needed to get dressed and check on her in the gym. Fast.

But when I caught a glimpse of myself in the mirror, with the white bathrobe and the Founding Father wig, I just felt helpless and kind of stupid. Because this wasn't just another costume, something I'd put on to make some in-your-face anti-fashion statement. Right at that moment I felt almost naked.

And I thought: *Okay, Tally, what exactly are you doing? Does Ava really need you to rescue her? She sure acted like she didn't. She was nice all afternoon—and her mom, too—but she's still Ava Seeley. She couldn't have changed that much over the last three days, right?*

Plus of course she had that awful photo of me.

I took off the wig. It was all damp inside, even from just a few minutes of wearing. Funny to think our country was founded by people with sweaty heads.

A knock on the door.

"Tally, can I come in?" Ms. Jordan called.

My stomach jumped. I tossed the wig in the closet and opened the door.

Ms. Jordan smiled a little as she walked inside the room and sat on the edge of Ava's bed. Her ponytail was droopy, and I could see her nose had gotten sunburned.

She glanced at my head with an almost-neutral expression. Not fiftieth percentile, more like sixty-fifth. "Some day you've had, Tally," she said quietly.

"Yeah," I said. "Some day."

"In case you're wondering, Mrs. Seeley already filled me

in on the hair situation. It's not the worst I've ever seen, if that's any consolation. Anyway, I hope you thanked her for the day. Ava, too."

"Oh, don't worry, I did! A bunch of times!"

"Good. I have to say, it made me so happy to see that display of class unity."

I didn't argue. I just watched her wipe some sweat from her brow with a crumpled tissue from her pocket. I could tell she was exhausted.

"All right, Tally, so here's the thing," she said. "I'm not going to ask about the hair dye. I'm going to assume you brought it with you from home."

"Thanks," I said, exhaling.

"But I have to tell you I'm not happy you did this on my watch. If your mom is upset—"

"She won't be!"

"Don't be so sure. Moms usually like their kids returned in the same condition as when they left. Dads, too, I'm guessing. Also, the principal is going to question my supervision."

"He is? But that's not fair!" I felt my face heating up. "I'll tell Mr. Barkley you had nothing to do with it! You were watching a movie!"

"That's the point. I probably shouldn't have let you stay in your room last night while the rest of us were downstairs."

"But I'm not a baby! I don't need a babysitter!" *Or a rescue dolphin.* "Ava was around! And Mrs. Seeley was right here on the floor too!"

"Well, yes. But clearly she wasn't paying attention every minute. And anyhow, Tally, you're my responsibility, not hers."

Oh, curses. Ms. Jordan was saying it wasn't just *my* problem; it was hers, too—and she could get in trouble for it. I remembered Mom saying that Ms. Jordan was a new teacher on probation, how any complaint could be a big deal for her.

The weird thing was how awful this made me feel. Somehow, during this trip, I'd changed my mind about my teacher. About a lot of things.

Maybe including Ava, too. Although that was complicated.

"So what *are* you going to do?" Ms. Jordan asked, sighing.

"About my hair?" I touched my head lightly. "I'm not sure. Mrs. Seeley said she knows someone who can fix it."

"I'm sure she does. But maybe your mom will want to weigh in with her own ideas. You should ask her."

I sighed. I was pretty positive that Mom's haircut place

didn't do Sour Apple Green. "Maybe I'll just shave it off and start all over."

"Don't." Ms. Jordan smiled tiredly. "There are better ways to express yourself, Tally. Try *words*, for example. If this town should teach you anything, it's that words are powerful tools."

Words.

Okay, I told myself. *So this is your cue to tell her about Ava.*

I took a deep breath. "Ms. Jordan? Can I talk to you about something? Not about hair."

"Sure. About what?"

I swallowed. "About Ava."

"What about her?" Ms. Jordan's ears perked up, like Spike's.

I knew I had to be careful here. I could just come right out and tell Ms. Jordan that Ava wasn't eating—but if that information got back to Mrs. Seeley, it could make everything more tense between them, and how would that help Ava? Knowing my track record lately, saying the wrong thing was a real possibility, and I couldn't take any chances.

Somehow, I knew, I had to communicate without blabbing. Not because I was afraid Ava would send the photo, but because I didn't want to betray her. That was it, crazy as it sounded. Despite everything I'd been through with Ava in the past few days, it felt as if we had a kind of connection. Not a friendship, whatever Ms. Jordan thought. And yes, it was complicated. But there was definitely some sort of crazy, random energy between us, almost like lightning.

I took an extra breath. "Ava went to the gym before, even though she wasn't feeling well. I tried to stop her, but she refused to listen."

"What do you mean by 'not feeling well'?" Ms. Jordan asked.

"Just . . . not feeling well."

She frowned. "Where's her mom?"

"Napping. Ava said not to wake her. She practically begged me not to."

My heart was pounding. Should I keep talking, or had I said enough? How much had Ms. Jordan noticed on her own? By now I had no idea how much the teachers knew about us—but it was definitely more than I'd realized.

I looked up. Ms. Jordan was staring at me. Wondering what I was thinking, maybe. Waiting for more words.

Footsteps, a click, and the door opened.

Ava walked into the room, pale and sweaty, holding a bottle of water. "Hey," she said softly, her eyes darting first at Ms. Jordan, then at me.

"Hello, Ava," Ms. Jordan said cheerily. "Tally was just filling me in on the lovely time you had today. I've never been to the National Zoo before. Was it fun?"

Ava pushed some hair out of her eyes. "Yeah, it was."

"Everything okay?"

"Uh-huh. Why wouldn't it be?"

"Tally said you weren't feeling well before."

Ava glanced at me. "She did? Well, yeah, I was hot and thirsty. But I'm good now."

"Great! And I'm glad you had a nice day, even though we all missed you both." Ms. Jordan stood. "Well, what I really need right now is a shower. See you downstairs for dinner in an hour?"

"Sure," Ava said.

"Sure," I echoed.

We watched our teacher leave the room.

Then Ava spun around. Her eyes glittered at me.

"Thanks, Tally," she spat out, stamped into the bathroom, and slammed the bathroom door behind her.

Sorry

AVA TOOK THE LONGEST SHOWER on record: thirty-five minutes. After that she probably used every bottle of conditioner on the sink, unzipped every pocket of her cosmetics bag, applied zit cream and sunscreen and every possible time-wasting product. Then she probably watched YouTube videos of baby hedgehogs as she blow-dried her hair. Finally, an hour after she'd walked in, she left the bathroom.

So I pounced. "Ava, I didn't tell Ms. Jordan *anything*," I said.

"Oh, I'm *sure*," she muttered.

"I didn't! I could have—I *wanted* to—but I didn't."

"Uh-huh."

"You don't believe me?"

"No, Tally. I don't believe you."

"Ava, really, why would I *lie*?"

She smirked. "Because you're scared of that photo. You don't care about me at all; you're scared people will see *you*."

"That's just wrong!" I sputtered. "I *do* care about you! And I'm really worried about you, okay? But I don't know what I'm supposed to do about it!"

"You're not supposed to 'do' anything. Can't you understand that, Tally? I don't need your good deeds. You don't have to adopt me, the way you adopted Caleb."

As soon as she said that, all the oxygen drained out of the room.

We stared at each other.

"Sorry," Ava murmured. Her face was red. "I didn't mean to say 'adopted.' It just came out."

"Well, don't apologize for it! It's not a dirty word! I told you—I'm *happy* I'm adopted. And that's not *all* I am, anyway. There's a lot more to me than being this Adopted Person!"

"Yeah, I know that, Tally. And there's a lot more to *me* than 'clonegirl.'"

"What?" My insides froze.

"Sonnet told Haley you called me that. Called us all that. It's a really mean word for someone, you know? Because we're not all one thing. Or all the *same* thing."

Oh, bleep, she's right. Because I don't know who Ava Seeley is, anyway. After the past three days, it's like she's a complete mystery.

And how could Sonnet have told Haley about that word? Even if it was unfair. And untrue.

"Sorry," I managed to say.

Ava shrugged, as if my apology didn't matter to her very much. "And when I said 'adopted,' all I meant was you're always acting like this big 'mom friend' to people. You treat Spider like such a baby. Like he's *your* baby."

I swallowed hard. Did everybody think I babied Spider? Poor Spider.

And really, what right did I have to take care of anybody? I was having enough trouble taking care of myself.

Ava tossed her suitcase on her bed. "*And* you're supposed to keep private stuff *private*."

"Which I did, I swear!" I protested. "Not because of that stupid photo, which I don't even care about! Because why should I? I can just cover up my hair until it's fixed."

I watched as she yanked clothes off hangers, throwing them randomly into her suitcase.

"Oh, but the photo, which I just now sent to certain people, isn't just about your *hair*, is it? It's about you *in my clothes*. You secretly wanting to look like me. All this time!"

She waved her phone at me so I could see the photo again. Of course I didn't look.

"You know what, Ava?" I thundered. "Let me tell you something: I *love* how I look! I think I'm beautiful and unique, and I'm really *proud* I'm so big and strong. I also think there's a lot more to me than how I look. And you know what else? I'm sorry I was ever nice to you!"

Her eyes filled with tears as she slammed her suitcase shut. "No, Tally, that's completely wrong. *I'm* sorry I was nice to *you*!"

After that, we didn't say another word to each other. A minute later, she took her suitcase and moved into her mom's room.

Optical Illusion

ALMOST AS SOON AS AVA had gone, someone was knocking.

"Tally?" Sonnet's voice called from out in the hall. "Are you okay?"

"Yup," I called through the door. *Even though you told Haley about the word "clonegirl."*

"Are you sure? Because I just got a weird photo. On my phone." Pause. "Can I come in?"

"Not now, okay?"

Pause.

"You sure you're all right, Tally?"

No. "Yeah, I'm fine. See you at dinner, Sonnet, okay?"

"Okay. I'll save you a seat."

"Thanks."

Pause.

"Tally, you're *sure*—"

"Positive! I'll be downstairs soon."

Except I couldn't bring myself to go to dinner. I just couldn't face everyone, not knowing who'd seen that photo of me on their phone. I mean, yes, I was used to people pointing at my outfits and laughing, but that sort of reaction was my *choice*. It was in my *control*. And the thing about that photo: Ava had taken away my choice. She'd captured me against my will; I was like her prisoner of war.

Plus, now people knew I called them clonegirls. That felt like another way I'd lost control. Not that I'd ever had control in the first place—but that word had made me *feel* as if I did, kind of.

I stayed in the room and watched TV. I don't even know what I watched, just happy people cracking jokes. And infomercials. Any minute I expected Ms. Jordan to knock on the door, asking to come in and sit on the edge of my bed for a sympathetic chat. But she never did, which was kind of disappointing, but also a relief.

I didn't sleep at all that night, even though I tried to imagine Spike again. By breakfast time I was starving. And the thought of sitting for six hours on the bus ride home, with none of Dad's Baked Goodies left to munch on, was unbearable. I needed to eat something, anything, to fortify myself for the trip.

But I still couldn't deal with the Thomas Jefferson. So I put on the purple newsboy cap, slipped into Ye Olde Apothecary Shoppe, and bought myself a couple of cardboardy granola bars. (When Mikel greeted me with "Hair she is, Miss Greenland, har har," I muttered "*Screaming Hairy Armadillo*" under my breath.)

We were supposed to board the bus at seven thirty, but I got on at seven fifteen, so I'd have my choice of seats. I took one way in the back, by a window, definitely giving off strong *don't sit with me* vibes.

A few minutes later, Derrick and Jamal took the seat in front of me. They were smirking and laughing, of course.

"Hey, Tally," Jamal said. "Can we ask you a question? How come you're wearing that—"

"I'm *not*," I growled. "It's an optical illusion." I tugged the cap lower to cover my ears.

A nanosecond later I realized I wasn't sure what he'd asked. Was it: How come you *are* wearing that hat? Or was it: How come you *were* wearing Ava's outfit in that photo? Because the thing was, I had no idea who'd seen the photo. Sonnet had, obviously, but who else? Maybe everyone. Maybe even the grown-ups, too. And people back home.

The bus was filling with kids, so I pretended to scratch some gum off the sole of my sneaker. Even with my head down, though, I could tell kids were peeking at me as they took their seats. Although Mia Gilroy didn't even try to act sneaky; she just stared at me and giggled behind her hand. Then she said something to Sydney, who announced, "I know, it's just so *fanny*; I *rally* don't know what to *thank*."

It was weird. I never used to care one hoot about Sad-nay's dumb opinion. So how come my insides turned to ice when she said that just now? What was going on with me, anyway?

A minute later Sonnet headed straight for the back of the bus. "Tally," she said, "why are you sitting back here, all by yourself? You should sit with me—"

And all your new friends—who know I called them clone-girls? Because you *told them? Maybe not.*

"I'm actually great back here," I informed her. "I just want to sleep. But thanks, Sonnet."

I pulled the cap over my eyes to show Sonnet that I meant it about sleeping. When she finally gave up and walked away, I stuck in the earplugs, not caring that they made me feel like I was underwater.

Even so, Spider took the adjoining seat. "You okay?" he asked quietly.

"Uh-huh." Because it was Spider, I took out the earplugs.

"I texted you a million times last night," he said. "You didn't answer."

"Sorry. I turned off my phone."

"Well, I was worried about you."

Spider was worried about *me*? That was strange to hear.

"So was Marco," he added.

I stared. "Really?"

"Of course." Spider rolled his eyes. "Come on, Tally. You *know* he has a crush on you, so don't be stupid."

I don't know what surprised me more: that Spider was acknowledging the crush situation with Marco, or that he'd called me stupid. The funny thing was, I felt happy about both. Although if Marco had seen that hideous photo, which he probably had, no way would the crush continue. For all I knew, it was over already.

I watched as Spider started reading a book he'd probably bought at the Museum of Natural History. It was about geodes, and it must have been fascinating, because in about two minutes he completely zoned out.

I poked his elbow. "You know what? I don't think you need the name Spider anymore."

"Yeah, Tally," he said calmly. "I'm not sure I ever did."

I stuck in the earplugs and napped for most of the way home.

Heads-Up

WHEN WE FINALLY PULLED INTO Eastview, Mom, Fiona, and Spike were all there in front of the school, waiting. As soon as I stepped off the bus, they practically crushed me in a sweaty family hug. Spike started licking my face and Fiona was laughing, but I caught Mom blinking really fast.

"What's wrong?" I demanded.

"Nothing." She was smiling. "You just look older somehow."

"It's the hair," Fiona said, sticking a finger under my cap.

My heart thumped. She couldn't see anything under my cap, could she? I thought I'd tucked it all in, but maybe not.

Although if any of my slime hair *was* poking out, why wasn't my whole family screaming in horror?

We piled into the car. Spike sat in my lap, nearly squishing me with doggy weight, shedding her smelly fur into my face. I felt my face relax into a smile, the first one I'd had in what felt like weeks.

At home there was a WELCOME HOME banner and a big chocolate-caramel cake Dad was still frosting in the kitchen. As soon as I sat at the table, I took off my cap.

And waited for a reaction.

None.

Dad brought the cake to the table and began slicing, while Mom passed out forks and plates. Spike was still in my lap, trying to snatch crumbs as we all began eating the cake, and nobody was saying a single word about my Swamp Thing hair. Which was definitely strange. No, worse than strange: unbearable.

Finally I couldn't stand it any longer. "So aren't you guys furious at me?" I blurted. "About the hair?"

Fiona licked her fork. "We're not allowed to be. Ms. Jordan won't let us."

"What?"

"Your teacher called us last night," Dad said. "She wanted

to give us the heads-up. Sorry," he added, when he realized that under the circumstances, he should have used a different expression.

Mom reached across the table to stroke my arm. "Honestly, Tally, it's not as bad as I imagined."

"It's worse than *I* thought," Fiona said.

"Fiona," Dad scolded. "How is that helpful?"

"Anyway," Mom continued, throwing Fiona a look, "Ms. Jordan asked us not to make too big a fuss about it. She said you were dealing with a lot on the trip, and that she saw a whole new side of you. A side that made her proud."

"*Proud?*" I repeated. "You sure you heard that right?"

Mom smiled. "Yes, as a matter of fact. You have no idea what she's talking about?"

I thought. Seriously, the trip had been a disaster. Caleb and I would be okay, but Sonnet had obviously made new best friends who all hated me. I'd wrecked my hair. I might have gotten Ms. Jordan in serious trouble. A nightmarish photo of me was on people's phones. I didn't know whose, but probably everyone's by now.

And Ava Seeley was officially my enemy. We'd always disliked each other before, but what had happened with Ms. Jordan—no, what Ava *thought* had happened—

meant we'd be battling each other forever, probably.

The worst part was that Ava had a really bad problem, and I'd done nothing to help her. Actually, I'd done the opposite of helping.

"No idea at all," I said.

Purple Streak

THE NEXT DAY WAS A staff development day, which meant teachers had meetings and kids had the day off from school. For me it meant going to Mom's hairdresser, Faustina, to get the KAPOW! stuff reversed. (This was Mom's idea, by the way; I didn't even mention Mrs. Seeley's hair person.)

"What did you *do*, Talia?" Faustina scolded me. "You had such nice, pretty dark hair!"

"I just wanted a change," I said.

"Change is for dollars!" She poured some goop on my head from a ketchup squeeze bottle. "And why do girls want to look like crayons? I'll tell you why. The internet!"

I burst into giggles. Mom, who was watching the whole thing, scolded me with her eyes, but she hid her laughing mouth behind a tissue.

And not for the first time, I considered how cool my parents were. Fiona, too. What if I'd ended up with Mrs. Seeley in my family? The thought of her, with her yolkless eggs and her colorless clothes, constantly in Ava's face, scolding and lecturing about competition in the work-place and carbs and French adverbs, almost made me sorry for Ava.

But as I watched my hair get changed back into dark brown, and then trimmed and shaped, I told myself not to fall into the trap of feeling sorry. Ava didn't deserve sorry. She was too mean for my feelings. And if I felt sorry for her, if I tried to be nice, she'd just turn on me again, take an awful photo, accuse me of talking behind her back. When I'd been *so careful* not to. Had been try-ing to be loyal. And, furthermore, had only been trying to *help* her.

"So?" Faustina was scowling at me. "You want a little crazy color, maybe?"

I glanced at Mom. "Can I? Just a little? *Please?*"

"A *little* color," Mom agreed. "But no bleach this time. Let's make it temporary. And no green."

"Purple!" I told Faustina.

"You'll look like a crayon," Faustina grumbled.

But she gave me a purple streak that looked truly amazing.

The next day was Saturday, and Caleb came over to walk Spike with me and talk about his new obsession: geodes. I was so happy to hang out with him like normal that I didn't even mention Marco.

At four o'clock Mrs. Nevins drove over to pick him up. She rolled down the window and poked her head out of the car. "Hurry, Caleb, or you'll be late," she called.

Then she smiled at me. "Caleb's going bowling with *Marco*," she announced proudly.

"Great," I said, thinking: *You must be so relieved that he's bowling with a male person.*

Caleb looked a little bit nervous. "Tally, I'd invite you to come with us, but—"

"You remembered I *detest* bowling. For which I thank you." I bowed. "See you Monday, Caleb."

"Yeah, Tally. Monday."

He got into his mom's car. "I like your hair, by the

way," he called out, just before they sped off.

I grinned. It was the first time he'd ever commented about how I looked.

As for Sonnet, I didn't see her all weekend. But she did send me a text: Hey. I just want you to know everyone is SO MAD at Ava for sending that photo :(. Nadia isn't speaking to her. And Haley says unless she apologizes to you (and means it!!!) she won't be friends with her anymore.

I wrote back: Cool. Thanks for telling me.

Sonnet: You should sit with us at lunch on Mon!!!

Me: Maybe I will.

Sonnet: Don't say maybe. Say YES!!!!

And I thought: *But you told Haley I called them clonegirls.*

Sonnet: I won't stop until you say YES, Tally.

I also thought: *Should I forgive you? It wasn't nice of you, even if it wasn't nice of me.*

Sonnet: I WILL HAUNT YOUR DREAMS

And then I thought: *She sure is stubborn about including me! Even if I used a stupid word about her new friends. Okay, fine—I give up.)*

Me: Fine, I will, okay? Now are you happy?!

Sonnet: :D :D :D

What We Learned

WHEN I CAME INTO THE kitchen for breakfast on Monday morning, Mom was there drinking coffee while Fiona read her phone and ate a Cinna-mmm muffin.

"Shouldn't you be at the bakery?" I asked Mom.

"On my way," she answered, smiling. "But I missed my baby like crazy last week, so I just wanted to see you off this morning. Oh, and give you this." She pushed a bakery box toward me.

"What's that for?"

"To bring to school for Ava and her mom. As our

thanks for taking care of you," she explained.

Oh, bleep.

Fiona looked up from her phone. "So Ava's mom turned out to be nice?"

"I guess," I muttered. "In a way. It's kind of complicated."

"Yeah?"

"I mean, she was nice to *me*. And she's not an evil person or anything. But."

Mom sipped her coffee. "But what?"

"I'm just glad we have the family we do," I said. "I really love us."

Mom's eyes filled. She reached across the table to smoosh me in a hug. "Me too, baby. And I'll always love Marisa for bringing you to us."

"So will I," I said, my voice wobbling.

"Aww," Fiona teased. "Such a touching scene, you guys." But she joined the hug also.

And while I was being smooshed by my mom and my sister, my brain was whirring. I couldn't give these pastries to Ava—if I did, she'd probably think I was taunting her or something. Plus I knew that Mrs. Seeley would disapprove of them, anyway. They weren't her idea of appropriate nutrition.

I finally pulled away. "But maybe we could give Ava and her mom something else? Like, I don't know. Roses?"

"Tally, roses are expensive," Mom said. "Besides, we're a bakery family, so this little gift from us is more personal. Just bring the box of goodies."

"And if the Seeleys don't appreciate it, tough," Fiona added.

What I did was bring the goodies to Ms. Jordan during homeroom.

"Oh, what are these for?" she asked.

"Just a thank you for the trip," I said. "And for calling my parents about the hair thing. It helped."

She smiled. "Well, the hair thing turned out gorgeous, Tally. I really like that bit of purple. And I hope the trip turned out okay for you in the end. I know there were some tricky moments."

The way she said this, I could tell she hadn't heard about the photo. Was that a good thing or a bad thing? I wasn't sure, but I wasn't going to tell her about it myself. No point making things even worse with Ava.

Later that morning, in social studies, Ms. Jordan greeted everyone as if she hadn't seen us in a month.

"I hope you all had time to recover from the trip," she said. "And before we proceed with our discussion of the *Federalist Papers*, I'd like us to take a few moments to reflect on what we learned in DC."

It was such a New Teacher thing to do. But Ms. Jordan was a really nice person, so I didn't resist.

"I learned that the National Zoo has a Screaming Hairy Armadillo," I said.

Ms. Jordan laughed. "Let's raise our hands, please, Tally."

I raised my hand. "*Screaming Hairy Armadillo*," I repeated. "Oh, and also, the Washington Monument is *not* five hundred fifty-five feet, five inches. At first I hated knowing that, but now I'm glad. I've decided it makes it seem more human."

Jamal's hand shot up. "I learned how the whispering gallery in the Capitol building works."

"I learned about the Skylab Four command module," Shanaya said. "And about the lunar rover."

"I learned the Supreme Court doesn't allow cell phones," Trey said. "Which is kind of stupid, although I guess they need it quiet."

Ava's hand waved high above her head, like a flag.

"Yes, Ava?" Ms. Jordan nodded at her, smiling.

Ava waited for everyone to look at her. Then she said, in a loud, clear voice: "I learned that there's no point trying to be nice to certain people, because whatever you do, they don't appreciate it. Also, if *everyone* thinks a certain person is freakish and crazy, it's probably true."

My mouth dropped open. Sonnet and Haley met my eyes.

"I learned some people can't admit they need help," I blurted.

"Okay," Ms. Jordan cut in. "Can we please—"

"And *some* people think they're Wonder Woman," Ava snapped.

"Nobody thinks that," I snapped back. *"Nobody."*

"Girls," Ms. Jordan said. "This is not a private discussion."

Ava smirked. "Well, good. Because Tally doesn't understand those *at all."*

"Ava, enough," Ms. Jordan said sharply. "I'd like a word with you after class. Tally, too."

"Me?" I said. "But what did *I* do?"

"*After* class. Not now," Ms. Jordan barked. Not sounding like a New Teacher at all.

When the bell rang, we waited for everyone to leave the room. Then Ava and I walked over to Ms. Jordan's desk.

"So," Ms. Jordan folded her arms across her chest. "What was *that* about?"

Ava tossed her head, reminding us about her perfect hair. "Nothing," she replied innocently. "You asked what we learned, and I was just answering the question."

"Come on, Ava, you knew what the question meant," I muttered.

"I agree," Ms. Jordan said, nodding. "Is there something you want to get off your chest, Ava? Because now is the time to do it. *Not* in the middle of class."

Ava shrugged. Ms. Jordan waited.

My heart banged. Were we going to stand here like this forever?

"Well, all right, then," Ms. Jordan finally said. "If you girls ever want to talk this out, I'm here for you. Or you can make an appointment with a guidance counselor. Whatever you two need to do to resolve this. But I do *not* want a repeat of today's class. Am I clear?"

"Sure," Ava said.

"Sure," I echoed.

"And Ava never apologized to you?" Sonnet was asking at lunch. "Not about what she said in class, *or* about the photo?"

"Nope," I said, waving across the cafeteria at Caleb as he took a seat with Marco.

"That's so horrible," Haley said. "I don't know what's up with her lately."

"In DC I tried talking to her about the food thing," Nadia said. "But she wouldn't listen. She said I was being jealous and bossy."

"Which you so aren't," Sonnet assured her.

"Well, even if she's grumpy from over-dieting, it doesn't give her the right to be nasty to her friends," Haley said. "And by the way, I love your hair, Tally."

"Yeah, the purple is awesome," Nadia said. "So was your mom mad at you after the trip?"

She meant about my Sour Apple hair. Ancient history! "Nah," I said. "Ms. Jordan called to warn her, so she was fine."

"And she's okay with the purple?"

"Yup."

"You're so lucky, Tally," Nadia said. "I wish my mom was as cool as yours."

"Yeah, she's pretty great." My eyes wandered over to the table where Caleb was sitting with Trey, Marco, Derrick, and Jamal. Right at that second, Marco looked up at me. I blushed.

"Do you think she'd talk to *my* mom?" Nadia was asking.

"About what?" I said.

"Some color. For me."

"I guess," I said. *Stop blushing.*

"My mom too?" Haley begged. "Pleeeeease, Tally?"

Sonnet grinned at me then, like *See? They can be nice, can't they? Don't you want to be their friend?*

That was when I finally focused: Nadia and Haley wanted the purple streak too. My hair color, maybe my haircut. And even if I wasn't using the word "clonegirl" anymore, I definitely didn't want them copying my hair.

"Anyway, I may have decided to shave my head," I declared. "I'm thinking of a henna design on my scalp. Maybe a Revolutionary War scene?"

"Tally, you're joking," Nadia said. "Aren't you?"

"I never joke. Ask Sonnet."

Sonnet turned pink. "Oh, Tally," she began, laughing.

Suddenly, on the other side of the lunchroom, there was a crash.

The Whole Truth

"AVA SEELEY JUST FAINTED!" ALTHEA was shouting. "Someone get the nurse!"

Nadia jumped up. "Omigod. Omigod."

"I'll go," I said, and started running down the hall to find Ms. Goswami, the school nurse.

But someone must have called her, because before I'd gotten halfway to her office, Ms. Goswami was running toward me. "Did you see it?" she asked breathlessly.

"No," I said. "Not this time."

"Excuse me?"

"I saw Ava faint on the seventh grade trip. After exercising."

"What kind of exercise?"

"Just sit-ups. But she's not eating."

"How do you know that?"

"I was her roommate. She threw away food—"

"Did you tell anyone? About the food and the fainting?"

"I couldn't! I wanted to but she made me promise!"

Ms. Goswami shot me a look. I knew it was an accusation: *You should have told someone, Tally. That was very poor judgment.*

By then we were in the lunchroom. Ava was already sitting up, smiling but looking as white as paper.

"I'm fine," she was saying to the crowd of kids standing around her. "I just got dizzy for a second."

Ms. Goswami knelt beside Ava, checked her pulse, felt her head, and murmured something in her ear. Ava nodded. Then Ms. Goswami slowly and carefully helped Ava stand and led her away, her arm around Ava's tiny shoulders.

The rest of us stood there.

"Whoa," Trey said. "That was scary, man."

"What's wrong with her?" Jamal asked.

Sonnet looked at me, as if I was the one who was supposed to answer.

And I probably could have:

She was over-exercising.

She felt hot.

She was super dehydrated.

It's a stomach thing.

Her parents are divorcing.

People faint all the time.

None of your business.

But none of these seemed like the whole truth—and anyway, right then I was too heartsick to say a word.

Ava didn't come to class for the rest of the day. And during music, some lady showed up to say I was "wanted" by Ms. Pressman in the guidance office. Which made me feel even more like a criminal than I already did.

And Ms. Pressman was pretty much the last person I wanted to see. She had a thing about "showing your feelings." Like she thought that unless you ugly-cried in her office, snot leaking out of your nose, you weren't telling her the truth.

As soon as I showed up, she led me into a tiny room and closed the door. "I guess you can figure out why I wanted to chat with you," she murmured, hypnotizing me with her sympathetic stare.

"It's about Ava's fainting, right?" I asked in a hollow whisper. "Is she okay?"

Ms. Pressman did a slow blink for an answer and rested her chin on her fists. "I heard this happened before?"

"Well, once. One time I know about."

I started talking. This time I didn't hold anything back. I told her about the cinnamon muffin, the meals in the garbage can, the notebook. All the exercising. Mrs. Seeley's comments about women's appearances, and carbs. Even the hangers. Even the divorce. Before I finished, the bell rang for the next period, but Ms. Pressman told me to stay. Maybe because I hadn't ugly-cried yet.

"So is Ava going to be okay?" I repeated.

"We're all very hopeful," she replied quietly. "One thing I'm sure of: She's going to get the best treatment out there. Anyway, thanks for all this background information. You've been so helpful, Tally."

But even though she was gazing at me with big, soft eyes, I knew she was lying. I hadn't been helpful at all, not really. I could have done more. Said more. Said anything.

A good roommate is more important than a friend.

But I hadn't been either one, had I? I'd pretended to be this nice, caring person, but the whole time I'd only been thinking about myself. Although not even about myself—about what *other* people thought about myself. And acting like this superhero dolphin, rescuing all the wrong people from drowning.

And then, thinking about water, I felt my eyes finally fill with tears.

A Bunch of Obelisks

AVA DIDN'T COME BACK TO school that week. Rumors swirled: She was in a hospital. She was living with her dad. She was being homeschooled. She was in a private school in DC. She was faking to get attention.

The following Monday, Ms. Pressman showed up in social studies.

"I want to share some news with you all about Ava," she said in her warm, slow, guidancey voice. "Speaking with some of you over the last week, I know you're aware that lately she hasn't been eating in a healthy way. Her parents have asked me to share with you that over the past few months, Ava has been struggling with an eating disorder, anorexia. Fortunately, there are caring experts who specialize in treating kids with this issue, helping them feel better about themselves and their bodies, and get healthy again. Ava's parents have found a wonderful treatment center for her, and that's where she'll be for a while. But she's planning to return to Eastview as soon as she can. And she's asked me to say she misses everybody."

"Omigod," Nadia said. Her face crumpled.

"Ava will be okay," Ms. Jordan said firmly. "And it's important that she knows we're all rooting for her. So I had this idea." She went into her closet and held up a giant glossy poster: a blowup of the class photo we took in front of the Lincoln Memorial. Everyone lined up in their ugly spirit tees. Everyone saying "dream." Me saying "cheese."

Ms. Jordan produced a bunch of colored Sharpies. "We'd like you to write a short note next to your picture," she said. "Just a simple, positive message. You know, like 'Thinking of you' or 'You can do it' or 'Go, Ava.' And then sign your name."

"Um," I said loudly. "That's not going to help, actually."

Everyone looked at me.

"Why not?" Nadia asked.

"Because it's such a lie," I said. "Everyone in the same stupid tee, smiling because we're supposed to. I mean, it's a nice picture and everything. But it's not who we *are*."

"Yeah?" Trey said. "So who are we, then?"

I shrugged. "I don't know, a bunch of obelisks. Really cool, but not just one thing, and not perfect anything. And definitely *not* all exactly the same."

"I see what you're getting at, Tally," Ms. Pressman said. "But—"

"Wait," I said. "I have an idea." I walked over to where Ms. Pressman held the poster, took it from her, and flipped it over against the whiteboard. Then I drew a line down the middle with a green Sharpie. In the left column I wrote: *WILAY*. In the right I wrote: *WILAM*.

"Who are Wilay and Wilam?" Marco asked.

I laughed. "It stands for What I Like About You and What I Like About Me. I'll go first." On the left side, which was all about Ava, I wrote:

Ava, I like your toughness, your smart brain, and the fact you don't snore.—Tally.

On the right I wrote:

I like my style, my height, my mathitude, and my squishy belly.—Tally.

I looked up. "Isn't *that* what we want to say to her? That we're *not* all the same; we're all weird in our own ways, and that's a *good* thing?"

Ms. Jordan was looking at me with shining eyes. "Tally, I love it," she said quietly.

"Okay, so who's next?" I asked, waving the Sharpie.

"Me," Marco said. Under *WILAY* he wrote: *I like how you aren't afraid of anything.* Under *WILAM* he wrote: *I'm a good brother. My nails grow really fast and so does my hair.*

"Sign your name," I told him. "So she knows who you are." Marco nodded, and wrote his name kind of like graffiti. It looked cool.

Then Nadia wrote: *Ava, you have the best smile. / I like my hair and my dimples. <3, Nadia*

Haley: *You are the strongest person I know, inside and out!!! / What I like about me is I have perfect pitch (according to my voice teacher). Also I like my freckles.*

Sonnet: *Ava, I like your pretty eyes and how you can be so sweet to your friends. / I like my shiny hair and that I'm getting braver about auditioning.*

Jamal: *Ava, I like how you always do your best and wear nice nail polish. / What I like about me is that I'm ambidextrous (mostly) and good at video games.*

Trey: *Ava, I think you're pretty and smart at everything, and someday you'll RUN THE WORLD. / What I like about me is my awesome sense of humor (haha) and the fact I can eat all the junk I want and never get cavities.*

Shanaya: *I like how fierce you are, Ava!! / I'm proud of my brown skin, my grades, and that I can do three somersaults in a row. (I think I'm fierce also—but maybe not as fierce as you. ;P)*

Sydney: *Ava, I think you're a really good athlete. / I like my neck.*

"My turn," Ms. Jordan said. She wrote: *Ava, I like your grit, determination, and competitiveness. You're the hardest worker I've ever seen, so KEEP AT IT. / What I like about me is that I love to learn. Also, since I started running, I have very strong leg muscles!!*

We kept going. When our class had finished, Ms. Jordan asked Ms. Pressman and me to deliver the poster to Mr. G, so he and his kids could add to it too. "Cool," Mr. G said when I explained it to him. "Two thumbs way up, Tally."

He wrote: *Ava, I like your determination and how much you care about people. / I like my beard, my quick reflexes in Ping-Pong, and how I geek out about the US Constitution!*

He handed the Sharpie to Caleb, who wrote in the WILAM column: *I like how fast I learn complicated things.*

Then he stopped. "I'm not sure what to say about Ava," he murmured.

"I know," I admitted. "She's not exactly . . ." I groped for the right word. "Simple."

Caleb's face lit up. And he wrote: *I like that you're complicated.*

Poster Girls

AT THE START OF EVERY school year, I have a hard time believing the weeks will pass. Somehow, though, they always do.

And seventh grade was speeding by. Maybe it was because I was so busy—Mr. Santiago had made me president of the Math Olympics team, and between the after-school practices and the Saturday meets at other schools, I barely had time for anything else. But I still hung out with Caleb some afternoons, and with Sonnet whenever I could. This meant also spending time with Nadia and

Haley, but they were both okay, I decided. Although I was still relieved they didn't get purple hair streaks.

As for Marco: He was also on the Math Olympics team, as a substitute, so we were together for most of the week. And considering how nice he was to Caleb, and how much he talked about his little brother . . . well, okay, I'll just say it. I realized the crush was a two-way thing. So we weren't "going out," technically, during that fall, but we were together a lot. It turned out he liked the same video games and movies as I did, so we always had plenty to talk about.

Oh yes, and I finally admitted to Sonnet that he was cute. *Preposterously* cute.

None of us heard anything from Ava, not even a thank-you for the poster. So part of me wondered if her mom had even shown it to her. Knowing Mrs. Seeley, I wouldn't have been surprised if she decided it was too messy. Or *inappropriate*, or some other Mrs. Seeley word.

I thought about writing to Ava, just to say hello, but then I remembered that we hadn't been on speaking terms when she left. I mean, I personally didn't feel angry anymore, but she'd never apologized about the phone photo, and I couldn't guess how she felt about me, even now. For all I knew, maybe she blamed me for ratting on her to the school nurse and the guidance counselor. I knew they'd spoken to other people besides me, but I was the *roommate*. The one who'd seen everything close-up. The one who knew secrets. So possibly Ava hated me even more than before.

But I didn't stop thinking about her. Wondering how she was, if she was getting better. Wondering when she'd be back. If she'd be back.

And then one Sunday, just after Thanksgiving, I was in the backyard throwing a Frisbee for Spike. Dad was there too, doing the last yard work before the winter, every once in a while taking a sip of cocoa from a mug he rested on our splintery old picnic table.

All of a sudden, Fiona came running over to us. She had a funny look on her face.

"Tally," she said. "We have visitors."

"Yeah? Who?"

"You're not going to believe it: *Ava Seeley*. And her *mom*." My stomach knotted.

"They're inside?" Dad asked, wiping his dirty hands on his jeans. "Where's Mom?"

"Making them tea." Fiona rolled her eyes. "Tally, I told them I wasn't sure where you were. If you want, I can say

I looked for you but you'd gone over to Spider's."

"You mean *Caleb*. No, it's okay," I told her. "You can tell Ava I'm here." My mind was racing. What would I say to her? What would she say to me? Would she look any different? What if she didn't?

Dad was watching my reaction. "Tally, don't feel obligated to hang out with her if you're not comfortable. Just say hello, be polite, and let us take over."

"Thanks, Dad." I turned to my sister. "But maybe could you ask her to come outside? Just her, I mean."

"You sure?" Fiona said. She looked worried. "Because it'll be harder to rescue you if you guys are out here by yourselves."

"I'm sure," I said. "Well, pretty sure."

Dad and Fiona exchanged glances, but Dad took his mug and they went inside. A moment later, there was Ava, walking toward me with a giant messenger bag across her body.

It took me a few seconds to register, but she looked older. Stronger. She was wearing normal jeans, not the super-skinny ones. And her face was maybe a little rounder. Just a bit.

"Hey," she said softly.

"Hey," I said, smiling, as Spike ran over to her to sniff her knees.

She bent over to ruffle the top of Spike's head, then smiled up at me.

I didn't know what to do next. But I decided, what the heck, I should hug her. So I did.

She hugged back. Under her fleece, her back didn't feel bony. Not that you could tell very much under clothing, but still.

"You look good," I said, as I pulled away.

"Yeah, thanks. I've gained seven pounds." She laughed. "And I'm not even feeling like a slug."

"That's great! So are you coming back to school?"

"Uh-huh. In a few weeks, I think. If my doctors say I'm ready."

"So that means you're all . . ."

"I'm better than before. But I'll always need to be careful, I guess. And have help." She shrugged. "That's okay."

"Great." What should I say next? I was starting to panic.

"I like your hair," Ava said. "But what happened to the purple streak?"

"I got tired of it. I mean, it's just hair; it's not who I *am* or anything." I threw the Frisbee for Spike. "Um, so did you ever get the poster?"

She smiled. "Yeah. I loved it."

"Really? And did you see all that stuff we wrote on the back?"

She nodded.

"That was my idea," I said, sort of shyly.

"I had a feeling. The way you signed it first." She grinned. "Actually, I brought the poster with me."

"You did? What for?"

"Well, if it's supposed to be our whole class, it isn't finished. I wanted to add something. Okay if we sit?"

"Sure," I said uncertainly.

We walked over to the old picnic table. Ava unzipped her bag and took out the poster, which she carefully unrolled and flipped over. Then she took out a blue marker.

"I got that WILAM idea from your magazine," I admitted.

"Yep, I know." I watched her write in the right column: *I like seeing how strong I am. How strong I can BE.*

"That's really great," I said.

"Thank you, Tally." She tucked some loose golden-brown hair behind her ear. "And I've had a lot of time to think about this, so I wanted to say thanks for a bunch of other things too."

I blinked. "What do you mean?"

"You know. Caring about how I was. Trying to help, even when I was so nasty to you. Not giving up."

"It's okay," I murmured. "I just wish I could have helped you more."

"You helped me more than anyone, Tally. So yeah. Thank you."

"You're welcome."

I didn't know what to say after that. So I pointed to the left column, What I Like About You. "That side is supposed to be about you too," I explained. "Because 'you' means 'you, Ava.'"

"Well, that's dumb!" Ava exclaimed with surprising force. "I'm not going to write about myself in *both* columns! So my WILAY column will be about *you*."

"Me?" I said.

"Yeah. We're going to argue about it?" She lifted her chin like she was ready for another fight.

Oh, bleep. Here we go again.

"No, of course not," I said quickly. "Go ahead, Ava. Write whatever you want."

She nodded. And then she picked up the marker and wrote, in her perfect, squarish handwriting:

I like how you were a good roommate—even before we were friends.

Acknowledgments

DEEPEST THANKS AGAIN TO MY brilliant editor, Alyson Heller, and to everyone at Aladdin/S&S—Mara Anastas, Fiona Simpson, Jodie Hockensmith, Michelle Leo, Tricia Lin, Chelsea Morgan, and Laura Lyn DiSiena. Karen Sherman, thanks for your sharp-eyed copyediting. Jenna Stempel, thank you for another gorgeous cover. Jill Grinberg, thanks for making another book come true. Always grateful to the whole team at Jill Grinberg Literary Management—Katelyn Detweiler, Cheryl Pientka, Denise St. Pierre, and Sophia Seidner.

Julie Chibbaro and Michelle Peña, thanks for reading an early draft with great care and sensitivity. Thanks to Carolyn Berger, LCSW, for talking to me about the wide-ranging experiences of kids in open adoptions. Frances Kellner, thank you for reading, offering insights about adoption—and most of all, for being my very dear friend.

A personal note: When I had an eating disorder in college, the subject was pretty much taboo. If there were experts around who could have helped me (and several of my classmates), I certainly didn't know about them. Somehow I found my way back to health, but mostly I was just lucky. As eating disorders become more common among tween girls, it's encouraging to note the range of treatments available. I'm deeply indebted to Kristin Lore, LCSW, for sharing her experience treating tween eating disorders, and for reading and commenting on an early draft. Kids need to know that caring professionals are out there—and that full recovery is possible.

As always, I'm beyond grateful for the loving support of my family: Josh, Lizzy, Alex, and Dani, and my partner-in-everything, Chris. Holly Doyne and George Rehm, we can never thank you enough for opening your arms. Luna and Ripley, thanks for letting me write (usually).

Resources

National Eating Disorder Association (NEDA)

Toll free helpline: 1-800-931-2237

nationaleatingdisorders.org

Provides programs for prevention, education, and access to treatment for individuals and families affected by eating disorders

Eating Disorder Referral and Information Center

edreferral.com

Dedicated to the prevention and treatment of eating disorders

Alliance for Eating Disorders Awareness

allianceforeatingdisorders.com

Helps families identify causes and symptoms of eating disorders

Academy for Eating Disorders (AED)

aedweb.org

An international source for information in the field of eating disorders

Adolescent Treatment Facilities for Eating Disorders

Clementine: A Monte Nido Affiliate for Adolescents

Locations in Florida, Oregon, and New York

855-900-2221

clementineprograms.com

Center for Discovery

Locations throughout the United States

866-482-3876

centerfordiscovery.com

PEBBLES

Every day that September, the four of us escaped out-doors. The weather was warm (a little too warm for fall, if you thought about it), and the cafeteria smelled gross, like melted cheddar cheese and disinfectant. So when the bell rang for lunch, we each grabbed something fast—a container of yogurt, a bag of chips, an apple—and ran out to the blacktop, where you could play basketball or run around, or just talk with your friends and breathe actual oxygen for thirty minutes.

Today was Omi's twelfth birthday, and we'd planned a surprise. While Max distracted her inside the cafeteria, Zara and I would run out to the blacktop and make a giant O out of pebbles. The O was my idea: her actual name was

Naomi-Jacinta Duarte Chavez, but we called her Omi for short.

And the thing about Omi was that she collected things from nature—seashells, bird feathers, stones in weird shapes and colors. So first we'd give Omi a birthday hug inside the O, and then we'd give her a little red pouch of chocolate pebbles—basically M&M's, but each one a different pebbly shape and color. It wouldn't be some generic babyish birthday celebration, with cupcakes for the whole class, like you did in elementary school. Just something personal and private, for our friends.

But what happened was, the exact second Zara and I stepped outside, Ms. Wardak, the lunch aide, blocked us. Usually she ignored us, and we ignored her back. Although not today, for some reason.

"Why are you girls out here?" she demanded. "You're supposed to go get lunch first."

"We know, but it's our friend's birthday," Zara said. "And we wanted to make her name out of pebbles."

"I'm sorry, *what*?" Ms. Wardak's whistle bounced on her chest.

"Just her first initial," I said.

"Out of *pebbles*?" Ms. Wardak asked. "That's a birthday present?"

Suddenly I was feeling a little sticky inside my fuzzy green sweater. We didn't have time for this conversation.

And we definitely didn't have time to explain seventh graders, if Ms. Wardak didn't understand things.

"It's not the *whole* present," I said quickly. "Just one little thing we wanted to do. And please, we really do need to hurry. Because our friend is coming out here any second, so."

Ms. Wardak sighed, like she didn't have the energy to argue that normal humans liked their presents pebble-free, and in boxes. "Fine. Just be sure you clean up the mess afterward, girls. I don't want any basketball players to trip."

"Oh, we won't be anywhere *near* the basketball hoop," Zara promised. "That's kind of the *opposite* of where we'll be. We're usually over where it's more private—"

I tugged her sleeve. Sometimes Zara didn't keep track of time very well. And anyway, I couldn't see a reason to share our lunchtime habits with Ms. Wardak.

We ran over to the far edge of the blacktop, where a strip of pebbles divided the ground into School and Not-School. Often during lunch my friends and I hung out here and just talked. Or sang (mostly that was Zara, who world-premiered her own compositions). Or pebble-hunted (mostly that was Omi, although sometimes me, too). One time Max and I joined a game called untag on the blacktop—not elementary school tag, but a whole different version, with crazy-complicated rules.

Although usually we hung out just the four of us, because I had band right after lunch, and we wouldn't be together the rest of the afternoon.

"Hey, Mila, look at this one—it's *literally purple*!" Zara shouted at me, as she crouched over the pebbles. "And ooh, this one sort of looks like an arrowhead! Or Oklahoma!"

"We don't have time to pick individually." I scooped up a handful of pebbles and started laying them out on the blacktop. "Come on, Zara, just help make the O."

"All right, all right," she pretend-grumbled. "How big?"

"I don't know, big enough for the four of us to stand in, so it's like an O for Omi. And also a Circle of Friendship." I'd thought of that just now; although I couldn't decide if it was cute or stupid.

Zara loved it. "Circle of Friendship! Oooh, that's perfect, Mila!" She began singing. *"Cir-cle of Friennndshhhii—"*

"Eek, hurry! I see them coming!"

Max and Omi were scurrying toward us, dodging a basketball. I hadn't seen it happen, but somehow, over the past minute, a game had started on the other end of the blacktop. The usual boys—Callum, Leo, Dante, and Tobias—crashing into each other. Banging the ball against the blacktop: *thwump, thwump*. Shouting, laughing, cheering, arguing.

"Over *here*!" I could hear Callum shouting at the

others. His voice was always the one that reached my ears. "Here! Throw it to *me*!"

We finished the O just as our friends arrived.

"HAPPPYYY BIIIRRTHDAAAY!" Zara shouted, opening her arms wide. "Look, Omi, we made you an O! For your initial, and also a literal Circle of Friendship! Which was Mila's idea," she added, catching my eye.

Omi clapped her hands and laughed. "I love it, you guys—it's beautiful! Thank you! I'll treasure it always!"

"Well, maybe not *always*," I said, grinning. "It's just a temporary work of art."

"Yeah, you know, like a sand sculpture," Max said. His big blue eyes were shining. "Or have you ever seen a Buddhist sand mandala? They use these different colors of sand—it's incredibly cool—and then they destroy it. On purpose." Max's mom was a Buddhist, so he knew all sorts of things like that.

"Huh," Zara said. "Fascinating, Max, but a little off topic." She pulled Omi inside the O. "Birthday hug! Everyone in!"

The four of us crowded into the O and threw our arms around each other. Because I was shorter than everyone else, I found myself in the middle of the hug, staring straight into Zara's collarbone. I'd never noticed it before, but she had a tiny snail-shaped freckle on her neck, two shades darker than her light brown skin.

"Okay, this is great, but promise you *won't* sing 'Happy Birthday'!" Omi was giggling.

"Sorry, Omi, it's required by headquarters," Zara replied.

She began singing in her strong, clear alto. Still hugging, Max and I joined in, a bit off-key, but so what. We were just up to "Happy birthday, dear Oooo-mi" when something brushed my shoulders. A hand.

Suddenly we were surrounded by the basketball boys—Callum, Leo, Dante, and Tobias. They'd locked arms around us and were singing along. Well, sort of singing.

"Happy birthday to yooouuu," Callum shouted into my hair. His breath on my neck made me shiver.

Now the song was over, but the hug was still happening, Callum's hand clamping the fuzz of my green sweater. The basketball boys smelled like boy sweat and pizza. I told myself to breathe slowly, through my teeth.

"What are you doing, Leo?" Zara laughed, a bit too loudly. Or maybe it just felt loud because she was so close. "Who said you could join the hug?"

"Don't be nasty—we just wanted to say happy birthday," Leo said. "Not to *you*, Zara. To Omi."

Zara flinched. It was a quick-enough flinch that maybe I was the only one who noticed. But then, I knew all about Zara's giant crush on Leo, who had wavy, sandy-colored hair, greenish eyes, and just a few freckles. He was cute, but in a *Hey, don't you think I'm cute?* sort of way.

I wriggled my shoulder, but Callum's hand was squeezing. And not leaving.

Now I could feel my armpits getting damp.

"Well, thanks, but I'm kind of getting smooshed here," Omi called out. "So if you guys wouldn't mind—"

"Okay, sorry!" Leo said. "Happy birthday, Omi! Bye!"

All at once, like a flock of birds, they took off for the basketball court.

Immediately my friends and I pulled apart, and I could breathe normally again.

"Okay, that was weird," I said, brushing boy molecules off the fuzz of my sweater.

"Oh, Mila, don't be such a baby," Zara said. "They were just being friendly."

I snorted. "You think getting smooshed like that is *friendly*?"

"Yeah, Zara," Max said. "You're only saying that because you like Leo."

Zara gave a short laugh. "All right, Max, I agree, the whole thing was *incredibly awkward*, but I thought it was kind of sweet. Didn't you, Omi?"

"I don't know, I guess," Omi said. "Maybe." She shrugged, but she was smiling. Also blushing.

Max's long hair was in his face, so I couldn't see his eyes. "Well, they wrecked the O," he muttered.

He was right: the pebbles were scattered everywhere. No more Circle of Friendship, or O for Omi.

"Dang," I said. "Well, we did promise Ms. Wardak we'd clear off the pebbles. So we should put them back now anyway."

"Who's Ms. Wardak?" Omi asked.

"You know. The lunch aide." I started kicking the pebbles over to the edge of the asphalt, and so did Max.

"Oh, who cares about *her*, Mila," Zara said impatiently. "She's not even a teacher, and she doesn't pay attention." She grabbed Omi's hand. "We have another present for you, and it's so much better! Look!"

Zara reached into her jeans pocket and pulled out the little red sack of chocolate pebbles.

Omi screamed. "Omigod, you guys, I love these! How did you know?"

"Because we're your best friends and we *do* pay attention," Zara replied, beaming.

I almost added that they were my idea. But I decided that wouldn't be best-friendly.

SWISH

Aside from lunch, when I could be with my friends, my best time at school was definitely band. I could be having a boring or awful or just not very fun day, and then as soon as I started playing my trumpet, it felt like the skies were opening up. And I had this feeling of endless space, no people or clouds or even buildings anywhere. Just big wide fields of grass and a blank blue sky. Sometimes when I was playing, I even saw the color blue.

I don't mean I *literally* saw the color blue. I mean it *felt* like the color blue. Calm and open, like it could go on forever.

Also, it just felt good to get really loud. Because all day long, teachers were telling us to be quiet. *No talking, no laughing, no whispering.* Sometimes our math teacher even complained about "loud sighing." So band was the one time of the day when you could let it out. *Should* let it out, the louder the better.

And after that weirdness today at lunch, I *needed* band.

But as soon as I took my chair in the trumpet section, I could tell something was up. People were standing around, chatting, laughing nervously, instead of warming up their instruments.

"What's going on?" I asked the kid to my right, Rowan Crawley.

"Section leaders getting announced," he muttered. "And that means Callum, of course."

"Dude," Dante agreed. He shoved Callum playfully.

Callum grinned.

I couldn't even look at him. Instead I took my trumpet out of its case, wiping it slowly and carefully with a little gray cloth. *Wipe, wipe, wipe.*

Ms. Fender tapped her music stand with her baton.

"Okay, people, here we go," she said. "I'm ready to announce this year's seventh grade band leaders."

Everyone stopped talking. Have you ever seen a tree full of chirping birds when a hawk or a fox appears? All of a sudden there isn't a peep. Just a sort of loud quiet. It was almost like that in the band room, except for chairs squeaking.

So it was weird that my heart was thumping. I mean,

I knew I played trumpet really well, and I'd even taken some private lessons over the summer with this cool high school girl named Emerson. But I didn't *really* think Ms. Fender would pick me for section leader. She was the kind of teacher who had special pets—people like Samira Spurlock on clarinet, and Annabel Cho on saxophone. Who I thought of as Pets Number One and Two.

And of the trumpet players, her favorite was Callum—Pet Number Three. We'd only been in seventh grade band for a couple of weeks, but already she'd made that clear. As soon as she handed out a new piece of music, she'd ask him to stand up and play it, not just for the trumpet section, but for the whole band. I'm not saying he wasn't a good player—and it wasn't that I was jealous. But I couldn't help wondering: Why was it always *him*?

"First I want to make clear that being chosen section leader is an honor, but also a big responsibility," Ms. Fender was saying. "So if you don't practice your instrument every day, you will quickly lose your position." She gave the whole band a stern look over her music stand. "We have a very ambitious program this year, and I'm going to need leaders I can count on. We *all* do."

Ms. Fender paused as she flipped her honey-colored hair over one shoulder. Music teachers know about timing.

And now she was smiling. "All right, then, without further ado: here are our seventh grade band leaders.

Please stand when I call your name. For clarinets, Samira Spurlock. For saxophones, Annabel Cho. For trumpets, Callum Burley—"

Hey, what a surprise. Pets Number One, Two, and Three.

Dante, who played trumpet, and Leo, who played sax, started cheering like they were at a basketball game. Tobias (trombone) actually whistled.

Callum stood, raking his floppy brown hair out of his dark brown eyes, blushing and smiling at his friends. And when he bowed—a sort of bow in quotation marks, as if he were wearing a tuxedo—his hand swished across my shoulder.

Had he noticed this? It was hard to imagine that he hadn't—my sweater was green and fuzzy, so unless his hand was expecting to collide with a Muppet or something, he should have been startled. Although he'd already touched my sweater during Omi's birthday hug, and actually, this hand swish was much quicker, more random, than the shoulder squeeze.

Still, it was the kind of contact that meant you should apologize. Even if he hadn't hurt my shoulder.

But when I looked at him, he didn't say anything or even glance in my direction. Probably he was focused on Ms. Fender, looking cool to his friends, making an impression on the entire band.

Who were all smiling at him, clapping. So of course that's what I did too.

About the Author

BARBARA DEE is the author of nine middle-grade novels published by Simon & Schuster, including *Everything I Know About You*, *Halfway Normal*, and *Star-Crossed*. Her books have received several starred reviews and been included on many best-of lists, including the ALA Rainbow List Top Ten, the Chicago Public Library Best of the Best, and the NCSS-CBC Notable Social Studies Trade Books for Young People. *Star-Crossed* was a Goodreads Choice Awards finalist, and *Halfway Normal* has been named to five state lists. Barbara lives with her family, including a naughty cat named Luna and a sweet rescue hound dog named Ripley, in Westchester County, New York.

Looking for another great book?
Find it
IN THE MIDDLE.

Fun, fantastic books for kids
in the in-be**TWEEN** age.

IntheMiddleBooks.com

SIMON & SCHUSTER
Children's Publishing   **f** /SimonKids   🐦 @SimonKids